HILLTOP ECHOES

ARTHUR ERI STEWART

SHIRES PRESS
4869 Main Street
P.O. Box 2200
Manchester Center, VT 05255
www.northshire.com

Hilltop Echoes

ISBN: 978-1-60571-026-6

ALSO BY ARTHUR ERI STEWART

The Highwayman
Jessie's Legacy
Last Haven Follies

Art Stewart

HILLTOP ECHOES

I will always remember waking up that morning. It was July 4, 1935 and I had been looking forward to this day for weeks. I was nine years old and it was my favorite day of any year. I think it was around five. I could hear Dad downstairs in the kitchen. He must have got back from milking. I guess that's what woke me up. I could see out of the window, and the sky through the big maple tree was so blue that it almost hurt my eyes. The big maple was around twenty feet from the house and I was upstairs in my sister Ena's old room. She is eleven years older than I, and I had moved into her room when she left for nursing school at a very young age.

I could hear the old cow bell ringing very softly in the morning breeze. It was up in the top of the big maple tree where I had hung it three years ago. My younger brother Ken and I used it for target practice with the 22 rifles. Ken was two years younger but he could shoot as well if not better than I. I closed my eyes for just a second to make this moment last. I had no idea that this moment would be with me forever.

It was time to get up. A wonderful day was ahead with fireworks and watermelon, homemade ice cream, hot dogs, burnt fingers and all that good stuff. I was up in two seconds and dressed. Dressing wasn't very hard; one pair of shorts and I was ready. I went down stairs and saw Mother at the stove and Dad coming out from the pantry where he had been straining the milk into the cooling pans. Just then Ken came into the kitchen wearing a big grin. Mom and Dad looked tired and were very quiet. Dad sat down at the kitchen table and Mother came over and put her hand on his shoulder and I knew something was wrong. Dad looked up and said, "Boys, Grammy died last night." Ken and I didn't know what to say. We just sat there. Our wonderful loving Grammy was gone. I felt a great loss and I am sure that Ken did too. Suddenly, the day didn't seem so wonderful and the sky not so blue. I didn't know what to say and Ken and I ate breakfast and went out to water the cows and our horse. I went to the barn and walked the two milk cows up to the well, pumped water into the tub and waited while they drank. I took them back to their stalls and Ken brought the horse and waited while he drank. Then we fed the chickens and we were done.

We went up and sat on the back porch and just looked at each other. What were we going to do? I kept thinking about the three big bags of fireworks that were under Dad's protection, but neither one of us dared mention them. There was a loud bang from the front of the house. We both ran around to the front and found Dad standing there with a little punk stick glowing in his hand and a small puff of smoke slowly moving across the still wet lawn. "You know, boys, Grammy always loved the Fourth of July, so I don't think she would mind if we set them off."

Even though we were sad, the rest of the day was fun. I don't think that it had really dawned on us that she was really gone. I was a little nervous around Dad as it started to dawn on me that he had lost his Mother. I had never thought of Grammy as Dad's mother, I always thought of her as my Grammy. The day went very fast and soon it was over. That year, 1935, will always stay with me as the start of growing more aware of the problems of life. I went to bed that night and lay awake, it seemed, forever. I wondered how Dad felt and if he could go to sleep or if he was awake, as I was. How did he feel? How did Mother feel? How did I feel? Who would teach me bible verses now that she was gone? Would she go to heaven? She'd had only one eye when she died.

Would she get it back in heaven? How did Ken feel? Was there a heaven? If not, what? Somewhere in the middle of all this confusion I fell asleep. July 4th, 1935, the day that, for the first time, I realized that I was not immortal.

Royalston was started in 1762. The town is named after The Hon. Isaac Royal, a citizen of Medford, Massachusetts. From 1743 to 1752 he served as deputy to the General Court. He was a man of great spirit for public enterprise, devoted to his King, and very generous for his time. He was chairman of the board of Charlestown and later served in the same position in Medford. He made a gift to the town of Royalston of twenty-five pounds sterling toward building a meeting house and a pulpit Bible which was used in the First Congregational Church for seventy-five years. By his will he also gave two hundred acres for school purposes and promised to give a full lot of land.

When the Revolution started, Isaac Royal could not be disloyal to his King and sailed for England in 1776, leaving his home. It was said to be one of the grandest estates in North America. He never returned and he died in Kensington, England, in 1781. The town of Royalston was incorporated in 1765.Without a doubt Royalston is one of the most beautiful towns in Massachusetts even today. The common has not changed at all in my lifetime.

I was born in Royalston, Massachusetts May 20, 1926 on the kitchen table, as were my two brothers and my sister. Don Verne Stewart is the oldest, born in 1911. My sister, Ena Virginia Stewart was born in 1915. Then me, Arthur Eri Stewart, born in 1926. Kenneth Luther Stewart, born in1928, is the youngest.

My father was Eri Shepardson Stewart, born in 1887. My mother, Bernice Iona Hager, was born in 1888. They were married in 1907. My grandfather on my father's side was Luther Emerson Stewart and on my mother's side, Arthur Hager. Luther died in 1914 and Arthur in 1953. Eri Stewart my father died in 1940. Bernice, my mother, died in 1974. Luther, my grandfather, was a Civil War veteran. He had been wounded twice, shot in the face at Antietam and in the foot at Cold Harbor. His leg was amputated below the knee and again above the knee due to infection. My grandfather Luther, as I have been told, was a hard man of the times. Times meaning his loss of leg and the pain of trying to carry on with an active life. I have read his diary that he kept during the Civil War, and my impression was that he came home a hard man. I wish that I had talked more to Dad about Luther. I think I would have learned much more than just what I picked up from other folks. I remember one story that is told about him deciding to make some home brew. I don't know how he got away with it as Grammy must have had a fit. Maybe that's the reason he acted as he did. He made a big production out of making it. The story goes, everything had to be just so. He bottled it and put it in the cellar that fall to mature. Later in the summer he had hired two men for help with the haying and they all were hustling to finish as it looked like the clouds were about to burst any second.

Luther said if they hurried and got the hay in before it rained he had a treat for them. Well, the last load was stowed in the barn and they all went up to the kitchen. Luther said that the home brew should be ready now and should be nice and cool from the cellar. Everyone was thirsty and the expectations were great. Well, he went down in the cellar and came up with two bottles and went over by the sink and opened one. I've been told that Grandma left the room in disgust. Well, he poured some into a glass, looked at it expectantly and took a big swallow.

They say he turned a little pale and spit it out into the sink and, in a loud voice, said that it wasn't fit for man or beast and proceeded to pour both down the sink. Then he got the rest and poured them all out too. Well, the boys got their water from the well and I've been told that the story went around town. I heard that most folks sort of figured that Luther wouldn't know if it tasted as it should or not, seeing as it would have been out of his realm of experience because, at least as far as anyone knew, Luther had never had alcohol in his life.

They say that it was about that time that something happened that might have made Luther, well maybe rethink a bit of life. He had a hired man that lived with them for a while and one morning he told him to put the bull in the back pasture. The young man said that he was afraid of the bull as it had been getting mean lately. Luther told him not to be so damn foolish and to get at it. Well jobs were scarce so he went down to the barn and hooked on to the bull's nose ring and started to lead him to the pasture. No one knows exactly what happened but the bull got loose and killed the young man. I've been told that Luther felt he should have listened to the young man and not sent him after that bull.

The farm consisted of 375 acres, of which about 45 were hay fields and gardens. On the left side of the farm we had a croquet ground that had two big maple trees. One at each end and it was a fairly level place. Every year we set up the wickets and played many a game with folks that came to visit. Ken and I loved to play and so did Sis. We set up a place years later when I moved to Cape Cod and played many games, some a little hot. We took the game rather seriously and had a few spats over the years. About 1933 Sis was becoming very interested in tennis and so were my father and mother. They thought it would help them with their weight. They were always trying to lose some and had used many diets in vain, at least that brought any lasting results. I remember one that was called the Grapefruit Diet. Mother said she thought it might work but she got awful sick of grapefruit. Now as to tennis, as all seemed to be interested, Dad decided he would build a court. Between the croquet court and the wall that bordered the woods, there was enough room for a full-size tennis court. I remember Dad and our hired man, Forest, digging up the top soil to lay a clay court. He had a horse drawn scoop to remove the top soil and then he put down clay. He bought a big hand drawn roller that you filled with water for weight and rolled the court dead level. When Dad decided to build something, it was done right and this job was no exception. He made a perfect regulation court that we used for years.

He installed poles ten feet high on all four sides and covered them with chicken wire to keep the balls in the court. I remember Aunty and Mother playing but don't seem to remember Dad playing very often. When Sis was home she had friends come to the farm to play quite often. We had the only court except for two up at Royalston center at the Lees and the Bullocks. They were very rich summer folks but they didn't have anything on us, I'll tell you. The farm really was quite a place and looked like some rich folks lived there. Ha, little did they know. Across the dirt road in the front of the house was the orchard with about 14 apple trees. Those trees were of great interest because my Grandfather Luther had been into grafting in a big way. Some of the trees had as many as four different kinds of apples on the same tree. Luther would take a McIntosh apple tree and, on some sides, there might be Baldwins and Northern Spys and on the other Red Astrachans. As a boy I thought this was amazing, and I couldn't figure it out until my father showed me Luther's books on grafting.

We raised produce of all kinds for the market. We also ate whatever was ready at the time. When it was pea picking time, we ate peas. Corn time every noon (dinner) we ate corn. Damn good but I was glad when it was out of season. We raised Howard 17 strawberries and shipped the plants all over the states. We dug the plants in the spring and packed them in wet moss and cardboard boxes and away they went. We picked hundreds of quarts of strawberries for the markets in Athol, which was about six miles away. They were placed in quart baskets, 40 baskets to a tray. Every night after picking, we would take the small miserable ones and make a meal of them. In August, we would take the horse and wagon and go damn near a mile up a cart path behind the barn to the best place I've ever seen for picking. Once there, we would pick blueberries most of the day. Mother would bring food for dinner with us. That blueberry picking was work, I'll tell you. We used milk pails hung around our necks on a rope harness to hold the pail so that you could pick with both hands. Strip is a better word then pick. The berries were enormous and in big clumps as the wet ground was just right for them to grow. I have never seen blueberries like that since, in the woods. Only the cultivated ones would hold a candle to those.

When we stopped picking, we would load all the pails and hook our old horse Jerry up, who had been tied in the shade, and head for home. This was the best part of the whole trip. It took about 30 minutes to get home. Even when we got so that we could see the house, we still had to go four-tenths of a mile across the field. The Farm wasn't called Level Acres for nothing. I didn't look forward to getting home as it meant we would be cleaning and sorting berries for a long time. Each year we made root beer and when we got home the first thing we did was pour a big drink of it. Boy was that good. I made it for my kids for years. It's getting hard to find the extract in the stores, and the last time we made it we had trouble finding it. Finally found it over in a little Harwich store. Guess what we would be having for supper? Blueberries, the runts too. Well, it really wasn't too bad. We would be picking over the berries for a couple of hours and then after supper we could listen to the radio, for we now had electricity. When I had been younger, we had a one-lung engine that we started up every night for two hours. It gave us direct current. It was housed in what we called the engine house, a small building 16' by 10'. The engine sat on a concrete floor and charged up a long row of wet cell batteries that stood on a shelf on the end wall. One gallon of gas every night would give us light for about two hours. When the engine ran out, the lights went very dim and we would either go to bed or light the oil lamps. Also, Dad's traps were stored there for his trap line he ran in colder weather. On a shelf at the side were jars of bait and, believe me, you didn't want to break open any of those. They would smell just awful.

Now that I think about it, it does seem strange that we had a telephone but no electricity. I don't know why, but the poles only carried telephone. I remember the meetings to get the power line run in to us. We had to get a certain number of families to pay a share to get it. It was hard as we were not very close together. We lived on Stewart Road. There were only three houses on it. Stewart Road was about three miles long, and we were the only ones on the road that would agree to pay for it. At the corner of the main road and Stewart was the old Tandy place. In 1800, it had been known as Cooks Tavern and was a stagecoach stop going to New Hampshire. The next house was the Sherwood's a mile up the road, then the Hartsons and that was it except for one house on Davis Hill Road which was about three hundred yards after Hartsons to the right. That was it for several miles. Going to the left from the corner of Stewart Road, the next house were our relatives the

Shepardsons, then only three more houses to the Athol town line. I remember those meetings very well. Mother thought that I had a fine singing voice so I had to sing one or two songs for the folks, accompanied by Mother on the piano. It was very common for this sort of entertainment at that time among country folks. Mother thought I was pretty good. God only knows how everyone else felt about it. Ken looked as pained as he could, I knew that he felt about the same as I would have if he had been singing. When I was ten I also took violin lessons from a nice man over in a town called Orange. I'll never know how Mother got the money to pay for the lessons, also she had to drive me over there, about twenty miles or so. I did very well but of course wouldn't practice enough. I played for the folks a few times and they suffered through it. In retrospect, it must have been awful.

Well, we finally got the power and it was wonderful. As time went on we bought a refrigerator, a radio and a real toaster and the lights never went dim. Before we got the power, our radio was a battery set and when the battery went flat it had to be recharged. We had to take it into Athol and it cost. It could only be charged so many times and then we had to buy a new one. There were long periods of radio silence.

Now we could hear Tom Mix, Superman, Little Orphan Annie and hear the world heavy weight boxing matches live. We listened to *Fibber McGee and Molly*; George Burns and Gracie Allen; *I Love a Mystery* with Jack, Doc and Reggie; and *Jack Armstrong, The All-American Boy.* We listened to Jack Benny, Bob Hope and Fred Allen. My mother listened to serials like Helen Trent, *The Guiding Light*, *One Man's Family* or *Ma Perkins*. These went on it seemed forever.

In the middle of the thirties we started to hear about all the problems in Europe and my mother said sure as "God made little green apples," it would mean war again. Ken and I did not pay very much attention to Mother but, of course, she was right. I did know that my folks were not big on Roosevelt as president, they liked Wendell Willkie. I remember the buttons, for president, you could pin on your coat. The radio was our link to the outside world. Entertainment wise it was wonderful and kept us connected to the real world.

Maybe four times a year, or so, we would go to the movies down in Athol. When we did, Dad tried to make it on a Saturday night as that meant for the same price you could see five acts of what was billed as RKO vaudeville. We loved it. We saw the beloved Will Rogers do his monologue and spin the rope. They also had a bank night where they would draw a name and someone would win a full set of dishes or money. We never did win but it sure was exciting. We only went when there was a real fine movie on. My dad loved the Johnson movies that Martin Johnson made with his wife, Osa in Africa, where they caught animals for the zoos. Osa carried a Savage 250/3000 rifle like Dad's, and there was a story that she had saved her husband's life from a charging elephant. It was true as we saw the whole thing in one of their movies. We saw the first full length animated cartoon. It was *Snow White and The Seven Dwarfs*. It was in 1937 and was tremendous. I don't think there has ever been another to equal it in color or animation.

As kids, we didn't have homework as such, unless we were having trouble with some subject, then your father or mother would help you at home. I was not good at learning and Dad was not good at teaching, schoolwork that is. Most nights after supper, Ken and I would listen to the radio until bedtime. The radio was a very important part of our lives in the thirties and forties.

Of all the things having electric power meant to my Mother I think that refrigeration meant the most. Before the electricity, Dad had bought an oak ice box that used blocks of ice. About every two weeks an ice truck would show up and we would get a block of ice. About fifty cents worth. The iceman sure didn't make very much on that sale, coming all the way out from Athol. We had to plan how we would use the ice so that we had enough for homemade ice cream. Mother would make the mix and Ken and I would take turns turning the handle on the big ice cream freezer, packed with ice, until it turned hard. She would pull the mixer and we would clean it off by tongue. She then sat the can in the ice box till time to serve. That method makes the best ice cream in the world.

The house was built sometime in 1800. When you looked at it from Stewart Road, the original house was one story. After Dad and Mother were married, four more rooms were added. Two down and two up. There were ten rooms in all when Grammy was alive, the old section was hers. There were stairs from her section and from ours. Her bedroom, upstairs had a big carved walnut bed that I looked at in awe. There were two holes drilled into the foot board. I was told they were drilled to take weights for Grandpa's stump. He suffered a lot of pain and had an awful lot of trouble with his wounds. Luther was 72 when he died and I have been told that he was out of his mind for quite a while and that he had to be committed as he could not be handled at home. On the wall in Grandma's living room there was a mounted woodcock, framed and under glass, that was the biggest I have ever seen. I was told that Luther had shot it years ago and had it mounted because of the size. Ken has it hanging on his wall which is only about a mile from where it was shot.

There was a woodshed behind the house and that's where the outhouse was. There wasn't even a covered walkway. We never had any plumbing as long as I lived there. There were two kitchens, one in the old section and one in the new. Both had a hand pump and used the same well. Every night, in the winter, the pump handle had to be raised to let the water down so that it wouldn't freeze overnight. Then in the morning we would get water out of the tank on the side of the kitchen stove and prime the pump. The water came to the house in lead pipes, of course today we all would have died of lead poisoning. I guess we were tougher then or something. Maybe it didn't hurt us because we didn't know it could. Makes sense to me.

One thing I will always remember is how cold it was in the winter when you went to the outhouse. In the summer, it was hot and smelled. No matter what the season, it was not a pleasant experience. One did not spend very much time there. We burned around fourteen cords of wood every year. The old section of the house had had a fireplace in Grammie's living room but it had been closed as long as I could remember. We heated the house with kitchen stoves that had big tanks on the side to heat the water for washing and whatever Mother needed hot water for.

When I was six in 1932, Mother and Dad celebrated their twenty-fifth wedding anniversary. I have the lists and autographs of all the friends and relatives that were there in a book Mother kept. They had one party given April 8th and again on April 9th. I don't know why. I was only six but I remember Mother coming in and getting us out of bed to see the folks for a short time. There was a big wedding cake and Mother kept the top ornament in her glass cabinet for years. In that book that I have there is a picture of the cake. They received seventy-eight silver dollars. Some of the couples gave a dollar. All are listed and the amounts shown. The book states what Mom and Dad did with the money and lists all the gifts. Havilland china plates two dozen, seven dollars, ensemble suits for Arthur and Kenneth, ten dollars--- Home Comfort Stove part payment, sixty-one. Looking through the names I know all but two on the list. At the two parties, there was a total of 55 silver dollars at the first and 62 at the second. At the first party, Mrs. Labonte made the cake. Mother doesn't say what they did with that money. I guess they had to do it in two parties or get a hall. That cake ornament was at the farm till the day we had the auction. I believe it fell apart.

The living rooms in both parts of the house had large stoves that burned chunks instead of split sticks. We had baths once a week in the kitchen standing in a tin tub. I hated the whole thing. Whenever I could I skipped it. The kitchen sink was cast iron and drained into what we called a cesspool buried in the ground. At least ours was. Grammie's just ran out into a ditch. Sometimes it smelled awful, especially when the weather was hot. The grass grew so high that you could hardly see where it was. Every once and awhile either Ken or I would step into it when running around the outside. On the wall beside the kitchen sink in our kitchen there was a mirror where Dad used to shave. I will always have this memory of him with his finger in a glass of water honing a Gillette razor blade. They were expensive and Dad sharpened them as long as he could. I don't know how many shaves he got out of one blade but it seemed to me he was always honing them before shaving.

There was a cellar under Grammie's kitchen and one under our kitchen. They were not connected. The center of the house had no cellar. To stay warm in the winter we had to set up boards held by stakes, about twenty inches out from the house and twenty-four inches high and filled with sawdust. Both cellars filled up about eight inches high with water every winter. The foundations were loose laid boulders and the water ran in easily. The stairs to Grammy's cellar were so steep that you had to be careful as you descended not to pitch forward into the dark. It was a dungeon, damp, dark, musty and altogether unappetizing. Under our side of the house it wasn't much better but had a better atmosphere or maybe smell. Houses smelled different when they had been heated by wood stoves for years.

We kept a model T Ford in an old shed down by the barn. Every winter we would cut hard wood for the next winter and piled it to cut up into stove lengths. In early fall Dad would start up the Ford, drive it up to the woodshed, jack up one back wheel and hook up the saw rig from a shaft put where the starting crank would go. We would borrow the saw rig from Dad's uncle, Luke Shepardson, who only lived about a mile away. The blade had no guard and it was very dangerous to use. Ken and I had heard the story of old man Pratt who used to help us, he lost his hand to the blade when Dad was running the saw. Mother tied a rope around it and they started up the old Buick and took him into Athol to the hospital. Mother always was very good in that sort of emergency. He lived without the hand but he never took wood away from the saw again. After the wood was cut up it had to be split for the cook stoves. For the living room stoves we cut big chunks. We had the fall to split and pile it in the woodshed. As soon as we were big enough Ken and I worked on it off and on.

Thinking of Mother and accidents makes me think of our old bob tail black cat. The damn thing just showed up one day. Of course, Ken and I wanted to keep it. And Mother liked him and Dad didn't care so we kept him. One day Dad was mowing the area we called the swale. It was hard mowing and the old horse really had to pull. He used to get white with sweat. It was wet and the grass was high and very coarse. Suddenly there was a howl and the cat burst out from in front of the cutter. He couldn't run and just kicked and yowled. Both back legs had damn near been cut off. Dad caught him and took him up to the house to Mother. Ken and I were ready to get Dad his gun to put him down but Mother decided to try and save him. She wrapped him up in a sheet with only one hind leg at a time out of the package. Dad went back to mowing and we went with her into Grammie's old kitchen. She laid him out on the pantry counter and I held him as best as I could. Mother brought iodine and all sorts of bandages and needles and thread. I had never seen anything like it. Blood everywhere and we had a very unhappy cat. She sewed him back together one hind leg after another. We kept him wrapped for several days then let him out and he limped just awful for about two weeks. After that no one would know he had ever had a problem. About a year later I cut my wrist to the bone and she told me to move my fingers and when I could she pulled it back together with adhesive tape. All I have is a big scar from it today.

Thinking of that cat makes me think of Mother's favorite old cat that she had for years. No one else liked the damn thing but Mother did. Well one time my oldest brother Don was sitting on the back porch and he could see Mother's cat sitting on the pasture wall down at the end of the field. He said to us boys, "Watch me make that damn old cat jump." It must have been three hundred yards and he had his 22. I don't know where he held but the cat fell off the wall liked he had been hit with a Mack truck. Don said, "Well I guess that scared him." We walked all the way down and he was right, it scared him, deader than hell. He had been hit plum center right in the head. We buried him and kept our mouths shut. Don told Mother about it about a year later when he got his courage up. She was not happy.

One of the never-ending jobs for Ken and I was to fill the wood box. When the addition was built Dad hired an old carpenter by the name of Buck Whitfield. The story goes that Mother was the bane of his life when he was working for us. Mother wanted a wood box that could be filled from the outside and she could get her wood from inside. At that time, all the wood boxes I saw were in the back hall which made it cold as hell when you had to get the wood. Mother didn't want that. After much deliberation and frustration Buck said he could do it if Mother would just leave him alone. The result was perfect. He built a box on the back porch about 4' high and 3' wide with a hinged let down door on the inside about 20"/30". You filled it from the outside and there was another door cut through on the inside. It was just perfect. It solved Mother's problem and ours too. It would hold enough for a day and we filled it every night. She also had Buck build a row of boxes with doors on the back porch for something. I never did figure what was supposed to go in there. The top of the boxes made a shelf about two feet deep and we piled our winter squash on it and covered them with old blankets to keep them from freezing. After a while it got too cold and we brought them into the house. Quite often we would keep several bags of potatoes on the porch to have them available for folks who would come to buy them. It was handy for us but the skunks also found it handy. Many a-morning, we would find a hole in one or more bags and chunks eaten out of the potatoes. There was an awful lot of skunks around and I think they passed the word that the porch was a damn good place to find food. Well this had to be solved and in our favor. Down in the barn Dad had several large wooden barrels. They were about twenty inches at the top and about forty inches high. He laid two of them on their sides balanced carefully over the edge of the porch. Then he put a spoon full of pig food (mash) in the barrels at the balance point and we waited till morning to see what would happen. In the morning, the two barrels were upright on the ground and each had a very angry skunk trapped inside. Now what to do. We had two skunks in two barrels and the challenge was to get rid of them without getting sprayed. We took the barrels one at a time and set them on the running board of the car. Then I held on to it out the window very nervously all the way to the end of the flat. The idea was to tip the barrel over and let the skunk walk away. Dad was going to stand there with the shotgun and if he started to turn to spray us he would shoot him. I think we trapped ten or so that year and only one was shot.

About that time a Mr. Waters came to visit us. Now he was a real know it all and told us that he could take care of those skunks without going all the way down the flat. He said there was nothing to it. He could charm them with a big wooden spoon and just rap them on the head and that would be the end of them. When he had arrived that morning, Mother told me later, he had been drinking a bit, maybe a lot because he knew he wouldn't get a drink at our house. Well Mother told him she had heard of this charming stunt but did not believe it would work. He told her if there was a skunk in the barrel tomorrow he would show her how it was done. Dad never said a word and I could hardly wait for morning. So, Mr. Waters got up and told us to watch him go to work. He carried the barrel very carefully out by the chicken coop, near the stone wall. He had borrowed a big wood spoon from Mother. He tipped it over, stepped back and started to hum in a low voice and waving the spoon in what he must have thought was a mesmerizing manner. He advanced on that poor little skunk. He got to what he must have thought was striking distance and raised the spoon for the killing blow. Well it never landed. That little skunk turned so fast that I never saw him move until I saw a stream of musk hit poor Mr. Waters in the chest. Mother, who had been watching out the kitchen window with great interest, clapped Dad on the shoulders and said. "Well that didn't work well did it?" Dad said maybe we should take him out some of his real old work clothes. Mother said she thought it would be a good idea if we waited till the skunk was gone. He seemed to be taking his own sweet time. He didn't seem to be upset at all because as he wandered around he kept looking back. After about five minutes he wandered off into the woods and Mother went out with some clothes for Waters. Just then the school bus came and we left. It was no wonder this episode got all over town, we told all six kids on the bus and I'm sure they told their parents. I think between Ken and I we must have told the whole school. When we got home that day the house smelled terrible and Mr. Waters was gone. I never asked why he had gone but I expect he smelled bad. The house smelled for a couple of weeks.

Later in life I used to wonder how we kids must have smelled on the bus. Most of us were farm kids and we didn't take showers every day as we do today. Once a week whether we needed them or not was the norm. I never noticed at the time as we all must have smelled about the same.

The back porch was 30' long and 12' deep. It was open rafters so that you could see the spiders. In the summer time the spiders loved it. They would spin their webs down from the rafters to the posts along the outside. We had the biggest spiders you ever saw. Ken and I would sit on the old glider and shoot them with BB guns. You can't believe how good we got. As we got older we switched to 22 rifles. When you hit them with the 22 they just vanished. When we got a little older we used to take the shotguns out and shoot at the bats in the early evening. Just about dusk they would fly by the back porch. I must tell the truth, as good as we were we still got damn few. I swear they could dodge the whole charge of shot. It was too expensive so we didn't do it often.

The farm house was home and I loved it always. Funny how things stay in your mind. There was a pot under every bed and in the winter when you emptied them there was a yellow hunk of ice. Believe me we used them. No one wanted to go out to the woodshed at 20 below as it was many nights. Dad had two sisters Aunt Ena, called Aunty, and Aunt Sadie. Those funny things I am referring to include Aunty in the summer when she was living with us. The first thing I would see of Aunty in the morning would be her coming down stairs going out the front door and emptying out the pot with a golden splash on the lawn. It seems strange now but things like that were just natural. My how we have changed. I remember reading just the other day about a wife who was complaining to "Dear Abby" about her husband who every once and awhile relieved himself from the back porch. "Dear Abby" predicted he would not amount to anything and that he was disgraceful. Well I don't know how graceful he was but I bet he felt free or is it relieved? I never could get that straight.

One very cold winter Ken and I were sleeping in the two upstairs bedrooms. It seemed that before morning most every night one of us would have to pee and it was damn cold and we were all tucked up in our feather beds. There was a pot under the beds but, if used, had to be emptied out the next morning. It seemed like a lot of work when there was a much better solution. We'd just go over to the window open it and push out the hinged storm window just a little and pee out the window. Now we were young and cold as hell so it was a long reach. One Saturday Dad was delivering mail and decided to stop at the house for dinner. He came in and said something to Mother in a low voice that we didn't hear and set down to eat. After a while he looked up and said there was something funny on the front of the house and he would like our opinion on it. We had no idea what he was talking about and we both were very interested to know what he had seen. After dinner, he got ready to leave and told us to put on our jackets and come out with him to the front. No wonder he wanted us to see this. The whole front of the house under the bedroom window was yellow and there were even some yellow icicles hanging off the window sill. He asked if I had any idea what caused such a colorful display. I made a mistake and said no. Father was upset to say the least and I think he would have sent me to cut a switch but for the snow being two feet deep by the lilac brush. Instead he informed me that we would have a discussion when he got home that night about lying. Ken just looked innocent and kept his mouth shut and made himself as small as he could. We had that talk and it was rather painful. The worst part was having to wait the rest of the day for him to come home. Well we never did that again at least in the winter. Just one of the pitfalls on the learning curve. Lesson, pee freezes when it's cold.

The barn was as old as Grammy's part of the house. All the beams that held it together were hand hewn chestnut. They were probably cut on what we called the Deacon's hill at the end of our road. When I was born the side hill at the end of our road was covered with great big white dead Chestnut trees. Now I mean big, 6' at the butt and very tall. They all had died from a blight before I was born. They have never come back but I hear that a few seem to be coming back blight free. I know where there are quite a few. I have been watching them for years but every one of them gets to be about twelve or fifteen inches high then dies. The loss of this tree should be considered a disaster. The big tie beams in the barn are about 16" square and solid as when they were cut. The barn is what we call barn framed and all siding is vertical. As you come in the big sliding door, on the left is the hay mow and if you go to the end of the barn and turn right you go up a ramp to the stalls for six cows. Also, there is a pen for a veal calf. There are lift doors in the floor so that the floor can be cleaned. The manure falls under the barn so it is accessible for use later on. The cows can be fed through sliding doors from the main floor. There is a passage between the hay storage and the horse stalls so that they also can be fed from the floor. Above the horse stall is a loft. Ken and I used to play up there. On the main floor is a big chest for grain. This grain box was a site of a lot of action. The big barn rats would get into the grain by chewing holes in the lid and many nights we would hold a rat killing party. Whoever was there would grab one of the clubs we kept by the barn door, the dog and sneak in quietly. We would snap on the light and raise the lid and look out! Rats going in all directions. The dog would almost always get one as they went over the edge of the chest and we usually got a couple more. You had to be careful as you could hit each other in all the excitement. It was an exercise in futility as the rat population never seemed to go down. I guess we did it for the hell of it. As far as I know no one ever tried to analyze why we did a lot of things. Just as well

I'm sure.

There was no water in the barn and we had to walk up to the well every day twice, to water the stock. In front to the left before the barn, were the chicken pens. Also, on the left in a shed were stalls for four horses. When we timbered off there was two teams in those. At the west end of Stewart Road was our mailbox and that of our neighbor the Hurd family who lived about a mile down the road from us. Our land abutted Shepardson's separated by a brook. In those days, it had brook trout all most all the time. They ran six inches up to about twelve and once and awhile after a big rain in the spring I would get one around fourteen. Ken and I spent many hours fishing that brook. The flood in 1938 and the new Tully Dam put an end to the trout. After the dam was put in I never caught another fish from that brook. The new dam saved the town of Athol from another flood and it was very successful for all of us, but it put an end to fishing in our home brook.

I went to school in a two-room school house for the first eight grades. It is still there. It has been turned into the Historical Society of Royalston. My eighth-grade class, (1940) was the last one to graduate from there. A new brick school was built in the field to the left. We had electricity in the old school but no plumbing. There were two outhouses, one for the boys on the left of the building, one for the girls, on the right. At the front on the left of the yard was the well with a tall pump. It froze up in the winter unless you let it drain so if you wanted a drink in the winter you had to prime it every time and then let it down again. The first floor consisted of a hallway running across the building with two doors leading into the one big class room. To the left of the hallway there was a stair leading up to another class room of the same dimensions. There would be one teacher down stairs for the first four grades and one upstairs for five through eight. It was quite a feat to teach four grades in one room. Remember you also had to keep the stove going. That in itself was not much fun. The stove was a very large cast iron monster that was surrounded by a tin reflector which also kept the kids from falling against the stove.

My teacher in the first four grades was Miss Huff. When we wanted to get her attention, we would raise our hands and repeat with a lot of breath: huff, huff. It used to drive her mad. She tried everything to stop us but even if I tried I would slip. Oh well I missed a lot of recesses staying inside as punishment. She was a very good teacher for the time and I got A's for the first four years, except for deportment. I met my best friend in school for the first time, Robert Smith (Bob). We were always in trouble and loved it. It was always great until our fathers got involved. Then it was not fun. Being switched was the way most everyone I knew in the country was punished. My Dad would send us out to cut a switch and if it was not in his judgment big enough or too limber, we were sent back to cut a better one. You learned to figure which one to cut. It hurt like hell but we were rather wild boys and it was just as well we did not get away with too much. I guess fathers and mothers would be arrested today for that kind of thing. I wonder if it hurt me in life, I doubt it. I never used a switch on my kids but I did spank a little, very little.

We had a principal that showed up around once a month, and if you were causing any problems, sometimes you were sent to have a talk with him. I had a few but found him to be the most boring man in God's green acre. My problem was not the talk. I just didn't want it to get back to Dad. Not many got to see the principal, I don't think the teachers liked to admit that they couldn't handle us. We had a school doctor, Dr. Hill, and a school nurse, Nurse McGowen. She was wonderful. We all loved her. We had TB tests once or twice. We'd get a shot and then they came back to see if we had it or if it was inflamed or something. If it didn't look right they would take you out of school to be x-rayed. There were some new kids that had moved in down on our road at the bottom of Doane's Hill. Two of them, a boy and a girl, had to leave school for a day as they showed positive. The rest of us were not very nice to them. There were a lot of people getting TB in those days and we didn't know much about it, but we did know better than to be mean to those kids. Years later I thought about what a little bastard I was to them. Well, they came back and were all right, but kids are mean.

Our school doctor, Dr. Hill, had a daughter Mary that was in my grade. She had black hair and was chubby to say the least, but oh boy was she smart. Bob and I hated her. She was what we called a teacher's pet. Well why not? If the teacher wanted an answer that most of us couldn't give, she always could. What a royal pain in the arse. I know now that it must have been very hard for her to be mixed with such a group of farm kids. She should have been in a private school. She was awkward and did not make friends with the other girls easily. God it must have been hard for her. Her folks were a little strange. She had a little brother that was a pretty good kid. He was also very bright but smart enough to keep it under his cap, so to speak. Her folks had a big house on the common and there was a rumor that her father had had a problem with opium. He had moved up here from someplace in a big city to start over. They didn't seem to have much money but none of us did either. It was just that her clothes were always threadbare. We all noticed but none of us were much better off.

Poor Mary. This is unbelievable but true. We had to give what the teacher called oral topics. You could pick any subject and give a little talk on it. I loved it. Once I got started you couldn't shut me up. The teacher always had to stop me. She would say "That's fine, Arthur, we must leave room for the others." Well one day it was Mary's turn and she had decided to talk on the Yellow-Bellied Sapsucker. Now by itself it sounds funny, but if you have a little lisp it is just too much. Of course, the kids were just about falling out of their seats. Miss Huff finally got us under control and Mary went on. All the time we were laughing she stood there with a sort of pained expression waiting for us to finish. She was really into her talk and looked disgusted with us. Oh God. She raised her arms to describe flight and her steins (panties) fell to the floor. There was a shocked silence. Without missing a beat Mary stepped out of her steins which were around her ankles, walked over to her desk, lifted the cover, placed them inside and returned to the front of the class and went on as if she was the only one in the class. The class was spellbound. I remember looking at Miss Huff and seeing her with a sort of dazed look on her face. Not a laugh or a giggle was heard. At noon, we all talked about it. Mary went home for dinner every day. This day she didn't come back for the rest of the day. You would think that she would have had a talk with her mother about new steins. Well I don't know if she did because about a year later she lost them again on the playground. This time the kids really laughed.

Well it was time for me to move up to the second floor. I had turned eleven so went into the fifth grade. For the next four years our teacher, Miss Elliot, was my first love. She was only twenty years old and I thought she was beautiful. She had bright red hair, a temper to match and I was in awe but of course at my age and being a boy that meant I would do all I could do to torment her. Later on in life I realized that I was just trying to have her notice me. Well I didn't have to worry about that. She noticed me just fine. I was in trouble from the first week. To get better acquainted she had a so-called joke day. The idea was that one at a time we could tell a favorite joke. Well I could hardly wait. I told a joke that my Mother and Father had told us.

It seemed that a little boy went to school for the first time and about ten o'clock he was sent home. His Mother asked him what he had done and he said that he didn't know. He said the teacher asked him to give his name and spell it for the class. So, he did.

"My name is Methyass Holebrook spelled M-E there's your me, T-H-Y there's your thy, there's your Methy, A-S-S, there's your ass, there's your Methyass. H-O-L-E there's your hole, there's your ass hole, B-R-O-O-K there's your brook, there's your Holebrook. There's your Methyass Holebook."

She couldn't send me home as I lived many miles away, but she could send a note to my Father. I was worried but Father seemed to take it pretty cool. Cool, a term I had never heard in that period of my life. It works though. Well, in retrospect, maybe there is something to be said for these new terms. Miss Maxine Elliot was a fine teacher. A few years after I had moved on to high school, she married a man who I thought the world of. He and I hunted birds together many times. For many years he was an alcoholic. Kenny Wilcox was his name. He became totally reformed at last after many years. I never heard Maxine say one word of complaint about him. She taught in schools all her life and all the town loved her. She and Kenny had twin daughters. They were beautiful girls. Bob and I were a lot of trouble to her and I guess others too.

I still remember one day I talked back several times to her when she tried to correct my behavior. In those days, corporal punishment was allowed. In fact, it was expected if you really misbehaved, which we did. She took me out into the back hall and gave me twelve strokes on the palm of my hand with a one-foot wood ruler. It hurt like hell but I just smiled. It's a wonder she didn't make it two dozen. I was not the only boy that drove her crazy. Dick Hurd, who lived just below us, brought a naughty magazine to school and we boys all sneaked out at recess to see it. Of course, Mary Hill saw us and told Miss Elliot. I can just see her doing it. No wonder all us boys hated her. By today's standards that magazine was as harmless as a glass of milk. When we went back into school Mary was sitting there in the front row with her hands folded in front of her, just waiting for the show. Too bad, Mary. Miss Elliott just told Dick to go out and stand in the hall. After she got us started on our work she told us to be quiet and left the room for the hall. Five minutes later she came back in with a very subdued Dick. It was never mentioned again but Dick had to carry a letter home to his parents. He cried on the way home. I knew he was in for a damn good licking. I remember when I got the ruler and told Grammy and she laughed too loud and Dad heard it. He wanted to know what was going on and, of course, it all came out. I had made a bad mistake. When Grammy laughed I thought it was funny and I laughed too, big mistake. Father did not think it was funny for me to think it was funny, I think. He took me to the kitchen, picked up the yard stick and proceeded to give me twelve more. Believe me, they were a lot worse then what I had received at school. Mother grinned but it didn't help.

At school, we had one hour for lunch. Not good, too much time to get into trouble. Every once and awhile a group of us boys would take off down an old road that led past the town dump. Most of the time we would keep running so that we could reach the Lawrence Brook. If we hurried we could get a quick swim and run like hell to make the bell. We had been caught doing this several times and it was strictly forbidden under penalties of being expelled or worse. Well this time the water was great and we could not get dressed fast enough to make it back. We were late. We ran as fast as we could but nothing could save us. We got to the school and ran up the stairs. When we turned the corner, there was Miss Elliott with a big stick about four feet long and about one inch thick. There was six of us and as we went by her she took a two-handed swing at our rear ends. She didn't miss any of us. I tried to pull my butt in but she got it. We were all black and blue on the backs of our upper thighs for several days. We had no recess or free time at lunch for two weeks. As far as I know Dad was never told. My brother was in the downstairs class and knew but he never said anything to Dad. My marks in those four grades were not good and I had a lot of trouble with math. My saving grace was the fact that I could read before I started school. When I was five my parents would have me show off for folks that came to the house. We had a deck of bird cards and I could name every bird. Everyone thought it was amazing. When I first did it I could only name a few but in no time, I could name every one and always right. I could not see what was so amazing. If I didn't know, I just read the name. I can't seem to remember when I couldn't read. I think that was why I got such fine marks in the first four grades. Even my math at that level was pretty good.

There was one person that I must mention as she was so very unusual. She was our music teacher. Her name was Leota Richards. She was a lady about fifty with a lovely wrinkled face and bright blue eyes. She loved music and we all sang our hearts out for her. Some of us were trying to learn to play the harmonica. I was trying but had no idea how. She could play and she started me on my way. She started a band and I was the only one who could not play at all. I had to stand beside Gordon Macanespie who had just come into town. His father was the new Congregational minister, and we did not like each other at all. All the girls thought he was just darling and that burned my arse. The worse part of it was that he could really play the harmonica, and I mean fancy, with little extra notes and such. God, I hated him. We would all stand up in a line about ten of us. All could play well but not me. So, as they all played I faked it, holding it up to my mouth and looking what I thought looked very musical, pretending to blow through it, then at home at night I would try to get a little bit of the idea of how to play it. I think I would have got away with it but for dear sweet Gordon. He kept saying in a loud voice that he couldn't hear me play. Of course he couldn't, I wasn't. Miss Richards, I figured out years later, probably knew what I was doing and she just ignored him. I was very uncomfortable, I really didn't want to get caught because I had been pretending right along that I could play. Well he wouldn't shut up and I sort of figured I would have to shut him up at recess. That did not happen. The parsonage was at the end of the playground and he ran home every time. It went on like that for a few days and I practiced every night. One Friday afternoon we were having a discussion in class about having Miss Richards help us to get some songs together that we could all play for the Royalston Day Celebration. Of course, I didn't keep my mouth shut and the next thing I knew I was asked by Miss Elliott to play a song that I liked. Up till then there wasn't a song that I could play. I could see Gordon looking pleased at the prospect of my imminent humiliation. I decided to fake it. I picked up the harmonica and made up a song. Amazingly it went very well and I kept going on not knowing how to finish it. I played single notes and it seemed that everyone liked it. Finally, I finished it off with a lovely soft trembling note and set down. You could have heard a hairpin fall. Miss Elliott said, "What is the name of that song Arthur?" Now what was I going to do? I said the first thing that came into my mind. "It's an old Scottish song called Bells," I replied. To myself I said, Please God don't let her ask me to play it again.

I never had any problem with Gordon after that so I must have got away with it. I learned to play very quickly after that.

It was about that time it was announced that a very famous person would be arriving. She was the former Empress Zita from the Austro-Hungarian Empire. She came to stay with Calvin Bullock on the common at his house that was called The Bastille. Calvin Bullock was our wealthiest resident but only was there during the summer. The Empress was in exile from the Nazi advance in Europe. Even today I still don't know why or who came up with the idea, but somehow it was decided that all the school children in Royalston should meet her. All of us kids were expected to be on our best behavior and to march over to The Bastille in a troupe and stand humbly in front of her and one at time sort of give a little bow. Well that didn't work for me. I just stood until she saw me and grinned and left. I wasn't the only boy that did that. We all caught hell when Miss Elliot got us back to the school. We were not used to bowing to anybody. To this day I can't believe we were asked to. I guess the town figured she was royalty and that was the proper way to act. Zita returned every summer for five years to the Bullock's. After that she moved to Quebec where she stayed for many years. This visit made the War seem a little more real to us, to see someone who was fleeing their home. The Bullocks owned several homes on the common and loved the town. When the 1938 hurricane struck, the Congregational Church on the common lost its steeple and it remained that way for two years as the congregation didn't have enough money to build a new one. Calvin Bullock donated a lot of the money to build a new one and will always be remembered for that and many other things that he did for the town.

I don't think I will ever forget the smell of wet wool mittens drying on the reflector around the stove in the winter. There was a steep hill across the stone wall on the left side of the school. The kids that lived in the center of town would bring their sleds and we would go sledding at noon. It was a very steep hill and you went fast. We had many a crash and some bruises. If you got hurt you must pretend it didn't hurt when you got back to school or we knew the teacher would put a stop to our sledding. We would all come in soaked. Wet feet and colds were common. All winter off and on we were sick with one thing or another. In my case I had ear problems. I would get earaches several days in a row and I remember my father holding his hand over my ear at night when it hurt. It seemed to help. We had a doctor that would come to see us when called. Doctor Coolidge was an old time Doc. At that time, all country doctors carried their own pharmacy, powders, elixirs, salves, etc. He would look in my ears and tell me I was doing fine and mix up a potion for me. He carried a fountain pen in his lapel pocket and he always mixed with it. I always noticed this and it bothered me. I always wondered what the last thing he used it for was. Mother said she was sure it was clean as it was certainly washed enough. Somehow it did not reassure me.

It was a good thing that doctors made house calls in those days or we would have had a very hard time seeing one. I learned to dislike him after I had a sore throat and the way to fix that, he said, was to take out my tonsils. Back then almost all of us lost them. My oldest brother Don had scared the hell out of me by telling me that a big dog sat by the operating table and as they were removed they were thrown to the dog who gobbled them down. Somehow, I didn't believe it but I was scared as hell. At the time, I was five years old. They took me to the Winchendon Hospital. I was used to having my temperature taken by mouth and my Mother told them so but they didn't believe it and tried to stick it up my arse. Big mistake. It took three nurses and one whose name was Miss Peabody got her watch broken. I found out later that she complained to Dad but he had no sympathy whatsoever. Dad carried me into the operating room and they tried to belt me to the table. I got away several times and then they slapped a mask over me and that smelled terrible. That's the last thing I remember and that's a hell of a way to go into surgery.

Nowadays the doctors would have recommended that I receive therapy for at least a year after being treated like that. Well maybe they would be right but I really don't think it did me any harm. I never forgave the doctor or the nurses though. I no sooner got home from the hospital then I got into trouble again. Dad was doing the assessing for the town and had the books out on the dining room table. Dad had gotten Ken and me a very young goat for a pet. He was great fun and gentle as a lamb. We sneaked him into the house one afternoon when Dad was working on the books. Dad was adding up and he had a hand crank adding machine. He had been working for hours and the floor was covered with long rolls of paper covered with the figures for assessing and setting the tax rate. We were getting ready to put the goat out in the barn as we had pushed it about enough, when he wandered into the living room. Dad had gone out to the kitchen to use the phone and the goat, being a goat, proceeded to eat the paper rolls. Not just a little but by the time we got there all of it. Hell, we didn't even know they ate paper. Well they do. He finished what he found on the floor and just as Dad came in took a bite out of a page in the town ledger. There was a yell and the sound of little heels on the hard wood floor as Dad chased him out of the house. Boy was he mad. He had not checked off all the figures and he needed those tapes. For a while I thought he was going to kill that damn goat. Mother thought it was funny as I caught her grinning in the kitchen later. Well we got through it but learned a lesson, goats eat paper, in fact they love it.

My gosh, how I seem to skip around. A second ago I was in the sixth grade, all of a sudden, I'm five years old again. It just shows that I have no idea what I am doing. My God I sound like I expected someone other than me to read this. What conceit. Well now that that little paper episode is out of my mind, I will try to go on. I will probably do the same thing again and again. If anyone ever reads this, I want them to know that I am aware of my lack of writing skills. I wouldn't want anyone to get the idea that I think I know what I'm doing.

Miss Elliott was the only teacher that I kept in touch with over the years. When she died I felt a great personal loss. I hope that everyone has a teacher like that in their life. I stopped to see her when she was in her late eighties and she was still beautiful.

Percy and Ruth Chace were very good friends of Mother and Dad and their oldest son Bob spent many summers at the farm with Ken and me. He was my age and was like a second brother to us. He lived and went to school in Athol. We did everything together all summer. We picked blueberries on our own to get money for 22s and shot gun ammo. 22 shots were twenty cents a box. A box held fifty. Long rifle was the best but was thirty-five cents a box so most of the time we used shorts. The 22 is very accurate and every boy in Royalston knew them well. We shot them by the hour at least till we ran out of ammo.

Ken and I used to pick blueberries out behind the barn on the side hill. One day we started to cross the pasture behind the barn and our milk cow decided that she didn't want us in her territory and tried to run us down. Well she did run us out of the field so I thought we better tell Mother before we tried to get by her again. Mother just laughed and told us we were sissies and she would show us how foolish we were. She marched down back of the barn and boldly started to walk by our old cow, but she wasn't having any of it at all and put her head down and came for Mother, who didn't back up one inch. She reached down and grabbed a hunk of slab wood that was laying there and just smacked the cow over the head with a loving, get out of here you damned old fool. Let me tell you we never had any problem with that cow again.

We raised a pig every year. Dad would come home with a little one in the spring and we would put it in the pen and take care of it until late fall. It would weigh about two thirty or so each year. When time came for butchering, that was always a big event for us kids. The day before, Dad would go up to Mr. Hartson's and borrow his big wooden tub and set it up in the barn under the hanging blocks. The next morning, he would half fill it with hot water. We would let the pig out and stick him and he would bleed to death. Sometimes we would put a trail of corn on the ground and he would gobble it up and walk into the barn and die right by the blocks. That was always a big help. Otherwise you would have to heave to get him into the barn. There was a stick that went from leg to leg held by a cut through the heal tendon and we would lift him up and dunk him in the hot water. We used old metal candle holders that had been sharpened at the base to scrape the hair off. I remember Don helping several times. Sis used to watch every once and a while with cousin My or a friend, it was quite an occasion. Dad was a very good butcher and several of the neighbors used to ask Dad for help when it came time to butcher. Dad would remove the hair and gut him and take the meat saw and cut the pig through the center of the back right through the center of the head. He always called the inspector of meat for the town for inspection as that was the law. At that time, every town had an inspector and the one I remember coming was old man Durrant. I don't know what he was looking for, but he would come in and talk with Dad and after a while he would go over and look at the two sides and take out his ink pad and stamp the pig with his acceptance mark.

Sometime in the next day or so, Dad would take the pig halves up to Grammy's old kitchen and lay them out on the pantry counter. It was usually November and there was no heat in the pantry. That's the way we took care of our meat. Every night when we had meat Dad would go into Grammy's kitchen and cut what we would eat for supper. The pig was cut up into large squares of fat and that was fried as bacon. The pig was never smoked and the ham was what we called fresh pork. I loved it and always will. I like cured ham but the pork chops, it's the best tasting meat you will ever have. I don't think the pig froze solid all winter but I never saw any spoiled meat. The bacon or fat that we cut into blocks was put into a barrel in the cellar in a brine and used all winter. We called it salt pork and if you ate it today it would probably kill you in a few short years. We just didn't know any better. Boy was it good.

There used to be a story going around about folks who had big families and only one pig. They would take a piece of salt pork to eat with their potatoes and tie a string around it. You would eat it with your bite of potatoes and swallow and then jerk it back up and pass it to the sister or brother on your right and so on until it got back to you and then you would start over again. You have to develop a sort of sense of humor for those sorts of tales, or are they just tales?

We were in the depression in the 30's and money came hard. As boys living out in the country, there was no way we could get any except by picking blueberries or such. My father, during strawberry picking season, hired folks to pick for him. He paid the pickers three cents a basket rounded off at the top. He paid Ken and me one cent a basket. When the season was at its peak, a good picker could pick a hundred baskets in a nine-hour day. Three dollars was not too bad for the time. It was back breaking work. If you wanted to make good money, you bent over with your legs straddling the row and only stood up to get a drink of water or to get more baskets. You would take about forty, piled one inside the other, with you and pick. The first picking would only last about three days so you can see we didn't have much of a chance to earn money. As kids, we would pick maybe thirty or forty apiece. Then that night we had to eat the damn things. Even to this day I can only eat strawberry shortcake. I would never pick one up and eat it by itself. Blueberries I can't stand in any fashion. My kids can't understand why, even when I try to explain it.

Once and awhile, Dad and I would go up to the creek to fish for suckers. At the right time, there was one deep hole that we got to by canoe, that we could fish for hours before they quit. They were big, some up to twenty-four inches. When they quit biting, we would put the canoe on the top of the old 1928 Buick and on the way home swing by Mrs. Whittfield's. She was a wonderful old lady and took in what we called state women. I guess some were a bit simple and I expect some just had no place to go, so the state took care of them. It was quite common for families in town to take care of folks like that. My father told me that the state or the town paid for their care. If anyone in town got into trouble at an advanced age, the town took care of them. Each town took care of their own people. That's the way welfare worked in those days for the most part. I still drive by the old Poor House that was in use years ago in Athol. Of course, it is no longer used and is falling down. When I was a kid I knew some of the old folks that lived there. I wonder if that was a better way to handle those sorts of problems? It seemed to work.

Well to get back to Mrs. Whittfield, she would pay me for as many fish as I had. Dad said she made fish chowder out of them for the ladies. It was funny, I always got the same amount if it was one fish or a dozen. It was always fifty cents. She would take me into her bedroom and by her bed there was a carved four-sided table with a little draw on each corner. Now you couldn't tell there was a drawer there if you didn't know. When she opened them, I could look inside and see lots of silver half dollars. As I write this I know right where that little table is. It's downstairs in my gun room, office combination and I have had that little table since 1949. With the Whittfields lived an old lady who we called Aunt Lucy. Her real name was Lucy Kesselhearth. She was a friend of theirs and was one of the family. I guess she must have fallen on hard times and the Whitfield's had taken her in. I thought the world of her. She wore boots, men's pants and denim jackets and tramped the woods hunting and fishing for the table and, I expect, for pleasure. She always carried a little 410 Harrington and Richardson single barrel shotgun whenever she was outdoors. Even when she worked in the garden she was armed. And when she died, somehow Dad ended up with that little gun and gave it to me. My darling brother, Ken, sold it when I was in the Marine Corp. I was angry at him about that for a long time. Mrs. Whittfield's father, Buck, lived with her also. He was the carpenter that did the work at our house. He was deaf as a doorpost. I couldn't understand him but Dad could carry on a conversation with him in a perfectly normal matter.

It was nice for us to be the sons of a man that everyone thought the world of. Everyone in town knew my dad and respected him. I remember when

Mrs. Whittfield told Dad that he was to be the executor of her estate when she died. They had no living relatives. As a kid I really liked them and looked forward to going up there with Dad. They lived in West Royalston on the Falls Road that started to the right at the bottom of Jacobs Ladder. They also had a man, Herb Graves, that lived with them. He ran the farm for them. He was about as bright as a lump of cordwood but good hearted. They gave him life tenancy, I think, in place of a salary. As a kid I never really knew but heard Mother and Dad talking about it and that's what they thought. The old Graves' place had burned down years ago and he had no place to go and no close relatives. He, like Aunt Lucy, was told to move in with the Whittfields. There was a lot of that sort of thing going on at that time. Just another way of looking out for folks who ended up alone.

The town had a lot of talent and several good actors. Every year at Royalston Day there would be a play put on by the folks in town. They did a great job and the plays were plays that had been performed on Broadway at some time. Dad was in some and I was in three that I remember. Some years it would be a Minstrel show and my best friend from school, Bob, and I would both be in them. I always looked forward to those days.

Now on Royalston Day there was a midway set up on the Town Hall lawn with all sorts of games run by town folks. One was Knock over the Kitty Cats. Three heavy canvas cats filled with sand and three baseballs. If you knocked them all off the shelf you won a cane or ash tray or whatever they had that year. Dad was very good at it and all the men would try to beat him. Dad loved this sort of thing. I remember young Walter Clark wanted to beat him in the worst way. Walter was trying to grow a mustache but he was very young and it wasn't doing very well. He came over to the booth and told Dad that he thought that he was man enough to beat him. Dad looked him over carefully and said, "Why, Walter, are you trying to grow a mustache?" Walter nodded and stepped up to throw the balls. Dad said, "Walter, what you do is every day you put a little cream on it and let the cat lick it off and it will grow in no time." Walter was quite flustered and missed his first ball. There's more to winning then just throwing the ball. Just another little bump in the learning curve.

Ken and I along with Bob spent many hours each summer day walking the dirt roads with our BB guns. The CCC crews had been working all over and had put in water holes. CCC stood for Civilian Conservation Corps. It was a make work program that our president, Mr. Franklin Delano Roosevelt, decided that, along with several other programs, would save the nation. I don't know about that, but they sure made a lot of water holes and it was a great place to shoot frogs. It was good for target practice for a couple of hours and you could wait a few days and come back and it was full of frogs again. The idea of those water holes was for fire protection, but most of our forest fires happened when it was very dry. By then the water holes were bone dry and all you had was a nicely fenced in mudhole. What the hell did I know, I was just a kid.

When Ken and I were about eight and ten, Dad was asked if he would take care of two large ponies for Mr. Cass who used them at the Athol Fair Grounds in the summer. At all the events, he would have them there to give kids pony rides. He paid Dad to take care of them. He paid for grain and what hay they ate. They had to be exercised. Well that was no problem for Ken and me. We rode those ponies all over town. We had them from middle of September to June. Some days in the winter, with first snow, we would get up and saddle them, load up and take off into the woods for most of the day. Mother would cut us a big fresh pork steak and we took matches, BB guns, fry pan, and a knife and we were off. A couple of times we sneaked the 22 rifles, hoping Mother wouldn't hear it when we shot. We would get up in the woods and find a place where a big pine tree had gone down in the hurricane in 1938. Very often when they went down they would take all the roots with them and it would make a wind break sometimes five or six feet in the air. We would build our fire in front of this wall and be really warm. We would play at whatever for a while till we were hungry then pull out our fry pan and cook dinner. After a while we would get bored and head for home. We had many great times with those two ponies.

We had a lot of adventures, some not well advised. One day we decided to ride the ponies up to Royalston center. Of course, we took our BB guns. It was a long trip. It was all dirt road up to the top of Doan's Hill, then tar to the center of town to the little store where we were planning to buy some penny candy. In all we would go about six miles. We didn't ask Mom because she would probably say no. Mothers are like that. We were beginning to find out that women were a puzzlement. It's part of a young man's growing up. We got to the store and rode around the common a bit and headed back home when low and behold who did we see but Mary Hill and Joan Gasman walking down the common. Without even talking it over, we dropped off our ponies and hid behind a white fence off to the side. They were not very far away but didn't see us at all. We both raised our BB guns and hit them in the rear end. Mary screamed and said she had been stung by a bee. So did Joan. They ran for Mary's house that was near and we got them both again. About then it dawned on us that our situation was apt to be reaching critical mass. We got on our ponies and were very nervous until we got around the corner. Then we almost fell off the ponies laughing. For a long time after that one of us would say the word bee and know just what the other would be thinking. How we ever got away with it is a miracle. If Dad or Mother had ever heard about it, we would have been doomed. The BB guns would have been gone till we were old men. I'm not proud of it but it sure was fun. I don't think I ever told that story before. I bet Ken hasn't either.

About a week after the attack of the bees, the state inspector of livestock came around to make sure that our cow was all right. They had to be checked for TB. The inspector gave her a shot and said he would be back in two days to check her. He came back and told us that the cow had come up positive for TB. That didn't mean she had it but checked out positive. Whatever the hell that meant. Well what it meant to us was the cow was doomed. At that time, we only had one cow which was probably a good thing as we might have lost another one too. I don't know where she went, but a truck arrived and they loaded her up and she was gone. Now we had a new problem, we had to buy another cow. At that time in our lives the only way we made any money was farming and the only way to get milk was from our own cow. I don't know how much Dad paid for a new cow but he was not happy about it at all. Now came the next step. The entire cow stable had to be white washed with white paint that would kill germs. Dad got out our sprayer we used to spray for bugs in the garden and mixed up the white powder. He and our hired man, Forest, sprayed for two days, two coats. It smelled awful but, in a few days, that disappeared. A few days later we got a Jersey cow who was just fresh and turned out to be a damn good milker.

Dad had a chance to go to work for the town as a foreman, bossing a road crew. It sure didn't pay much, but times were hard. Every once and awhile someone would come down the road looking for a drink of water and maybe a meal if they hit the right house. Our house was always the right house. Even though we had no job for them, we could always give them something to eat. Mother was very careful and the shotgun was right there behind the back door, but I never saw any problem with these men. They were just discouraged and hungry. Some were quite young and others rather old. Every age was in trouble in those days. They would eat, thank Mother and go up the road. I never saw the same man twice that I remember. If you have seen this sort of thing once in your life you will never forget the look of desperation and lack of hope that you could see in their faces.

The town hired local men to paint gypsy moths. They would come down the road on foot with long poles with a brush on the end and would dip the brush into pails of creosote and paint the eggs of the moths to kill them. This was very bad at times for the trees and you could see paths going through the woods thousands of yards wide with not a leaf on a tree. Many times, it killed the trees permanently. It must have been a very tiresome job but it was better than nothing. We knew most everyone on those crews and they always stopped to say hello to Dad.

Dad did run a road crew that summer and into the fall that year.

We cut the timbre on both sides of the field in 1935 and 1936. We cut the hill behind the barn first, about one hundred acres. The timbre was prime and we hired Mr. Taft from Orange to bring his rig to cut up the logs into boards. All our timbre was cut into boards as we were going to sell to Tyler Sash and Window in Athol and that's the way they wanted it. Dad hired men to cut and haul the logs to skid piles right by the mill site so that the men could roll them right onto the carriage that took them into the blade. It was really something to see that mill arrive. Old man Taft, as we called him, arrived one morning in his 1926 four door Rolls Royce touring car. Ken and I thought it was really something. He drove into the yard blowing the horn that was mounted on the outside of the car, by squeezing a big rubber ball fixed to the end of a big shiny horn. It was a fine fall day and he had the top down. What a car, and he kept it spotless. He told Dad that the mill would be here late tomorrow as it was on its way. He and Dad went to make sure there would be room so he could get saw rig up the hill through the woods on an old cart path. Of course, Ken and I had no idea what was coming. The next day about one o'clock we looked up the road and here came a six-horse team pulling a great long metal tank on two very big wagons. We had never seen a six-horse team before. We had seen four-horse teams but never a six-horse. I was fascinated. The horses were beauties all gussied up and stepping proud. I still didn't know what the hell that big tank was.

Well, you have properly guessed the mill was going to be run by steam. I had never seen anything run by steam before. They got it set up in front of the ramps we had set up to hold the logs. We had been cutting for a while and were ready to start hauling as needed to keep the ramp full. We needed snow to keep the ramps full and it was supposed to snow any time now. We hauled the logs on wooden sleds that we would shoe like you would a horse except we used long wooden runners held on by drilling inch-and-a-quarter holes through and into the wood stringers and locking them on with wood pegs. Of course, the shoes were all hard wood. They had to be reshod every two weeks or so as they would wear fast. The loads on the sleds were very heavy and it was a sight to see the horses break free the load and get it started to the ramps. It took a well-trained strong team for this kind of work. After a while, as time went on, the loads were further and further away and it was quite dangerous as the paths got steeper. The teamster had to have complete control of his team or the load could get away from him on the hills. Boy those horses were good. To see them hold back the load was a very thrilling sight for a boy who knew horses and loved them. There was one team in the spare stalls and another one was due in as soon as it snowed.

Well it snowed all right, about eight inches. Two days later Walter Shine came with his sled and his house which was on it. This was the way Walter made his living. He hired on with his team, sled and brought his house to live in. He didn't own a car so he stayed on the job for the whole winter or as long as needed. He was one of the nicest men I ever met. Mother would have him up to the house for supper about once a week. He was only about five feet tall. He was about fifty and had snow white hair with bright blue eyes and treated his horses like they were his family. It's a good thing because Dad wouldn't stand for anyone treating their teams cruelly. Every once and awhile I would go down to see him after supper just to talk. The little house he'd sledded in was about eight feet wide and ten feet long. There was a built-in cot across the back, a table, a stove, two chairs and a shelf for an oil lamp and wash basin. It was always warm and he kept it clean and always as neat as his horses. The house was set in front of the barn right by the shed where we had horse stalls. With his pair there was four horses stalled there. Just knowing Mr. Shine was a real treat.

When he worked you always got a full day, work plus! One Saturday night Dad said we were going to go to the movies and Mother said we should take Walter with us. He was very reluctant to go at first, I don't think he had seen a talking movie in his life. I remember all of us getting into the car and under the blankets as it was very cold. Cars had no heat at that time. He brought his big flashlight and we were off. The movie was The Fighting 69th with James Cagney and had a lot of battle sequences that were rough. I thought Walter was going to go through the roof. I was sitting beside him and I think he was almost scared out of his mind. He became rather verbal at times and kept making suggestions to the actors. Of course, being a kid, I was embarrassed but it didn't seem to bother Mother or Dad. I think they got a kick out of him. Well he got thru it but would not go with us again when we went in the spring. I must confess that movie scared Ken and I but we didn't let Walter know. On the way home, he kept saying he had never seen anything like it before and he didn't care if he never did again.

I wish I could see that mill work today. What a machine. It didn't make very much noise. Mostly just the sound of the saw going through the logs and once and a while he'd blow the whistle. There was another little saw run from a belt from the main engine and that was where the sides of the boards that were waste were cut up for stickers. These were used to put between the rows of boards that were piled up maybe eight feet or so. The stickers were used so that the air would circulate between the rows and dry the wood. Dad decided that he would truck his own lumber to Athol Tyler and Sash. He bought a 1929 Netco truck and the next fall after the wood was air dried he trucked it to Athol. That truck when loaded was very slow, and I went with him many times as most of the trucking was done on Saturdays. I guess some was trucked during the week when I was in school. I remember that a new law was passed by the state and Dad had to buy this black box that he attached to the steering wheel and four hooded black boxes that he bolted to the front and back of the truck. When you turned left or right you had to move a shiny handle that stuck up out of the inside box, in the direction you were turning and an arrow was lighted. I was quite impressed with it. My goodness we were getting modern. I loved to go to Athol in that big old Netco truck. I wish the cab had been heated.

Thank God we cut when we did before the hurricane. I never knew why but Mr. Taft ran the second mill from a gas engine and it made a lot more noise than steam. When they moved the saw rig into the woods on the other side of the field, they left the boiler. The last time I looked I couldn't see it. I guess Mr. Taft knew he wasn't going to use it again. As time went by, Ken and I could see it up on the hill. It must have been at least two thousand yards from the house. One day Ken and I were shooting off the back porch and I said I wonder if I could hit that big boiler. I tried and tried but could not find the right elevation. Ken said let him try so I did. Up on the hill in line with the boiler you could see a rock with a white face. Ken lined up on that and hit the boiler with a loud ring. Boy that was great, it really rang when it was hit so no one could doubt it. We were using 22 shorts and that was the only damn thing we could hit it with every time. Over the next ten years we won quite a bit of money on that shot. We nailed our older brother Don and some of his hunting buddies by betting him a quarter that we could hit it and they would laugh at us and take the bet. They weren't very bright if they thought we didn't have it in the bag. We never told anyone where we held and the rock was very small and no one ever made the boiler ring except us as far as I know.

Near that rock off to the right side there is a lovely spring with nice cool water clean as a hound's tooth. Ken and I always thought it would be wonderful to pipe it down to the barn the same as the Shepardsons did for their barn. I talked to Dad about it once but he was not that enthusiastic. When hunting up on the hill I've had many a drink from that spring for me and the dog. A good spring is a beautiful thing. Later on, the brush grew up and we lost the aiming spot, but I bet that boiler is still there, or maybe just a pile of rust. Last year I looked up there thinking of those days and nothing looks familiar. The skies don't even seem to be as blue as I remembered.

I think it was about this time that Dad came home and said that he wanted to take a vacation. I really didn't know what that was, I had never seen one. There was a little dirt road up past Hartson's. About a mile up that road at the top of Davis Hill there was a little cottage where people by the name of Hogsetts spent their summers. They thought the world of Dad and bought produce from him at the farm. Dad said that they owned an old house on Cape Cod and told Dad he could use it anytime. He said he thought that seeing we had cut off the timbre this year maybe sometime this summer he could take a week off and go to the Cape. Ken and I were so excited, I think he was sorry he had told us so soon. Our hired man Forest could take care of the stock and keep the gardens weeded and we could go. We left the first week in August. The Cape house was old alright but it was ok for us. It was in Sagamore right on the beach and lucky to be there as on both sides were wrecks of other places that had been flooded out. Dad and Mom got Percy and Ruth Chase, their friends, to come with us and Ken and I had a great time. Bob Chase, our friend, came too.

Our older sister came too. The one thing I remember very well was Sis embarrassing herself. She got time off and came with us. We rented an old rowboat to play and dive off to find sea clams that we could see on the bottom. A nice man by the name of Mr. Mandigo had one that was anchored so that at low tide you could walk out to it. Dad, Sis, Ken and I, along with Mr. Mandigo, were walking out to the boat at low tide. It must have been damn near a half mile out. I didn't think we would ever get there. Sis was enjoying herself greatly and teasing us all when she happened to look up and saw a fat woman sitting on the boat like she was a fixture. Sis said, "I wonder when that big fat woman will get off our boat." No one said anything for a minute. After a little pause Mr. Mandigo said, "I guess she'll get off when we get there, she's my wife." Poor Sis, she didn't know what to say after that and chose to say nothing. We didn't let her forget that slip for ages. We had a wonderful week and I loved the Cape, never dreaming I would be living there someday. We went to the Cape one more time two years later.

The 1938 hurricane was a very traumatic experience for us all. In those days, there was no warning from anyone. We had had an awful lot of rain for two days and the flooding was very prevalent. Athol was having trouble and the brooks were overflowing everywhere. It started to blow in the morning and kept increasing till the house shook. Then it got a whole lot worse. We thought the house was going to come apart. We were standing by the kitchen window looking out toward the left side of the flat when the two hen houses picked up and exploded with chickens and boards everywhere. We were looking past that when suddenly the timbre on the side hill just all laid down. Everywhere we looked the trees were going down

The big maples stayed up and we prayed they would make it. All of us were afraid that day. There were three Balm-of-Gilead trees that were very soft down by the old garage and we thought they would go at any minute, but they just lost limbs and looked all torn up. I didn't want to lose them as they were the only ones I had ever seen and they fascinated me. They are very old trees and are mentioned in the Bible. The ends of the branches have buds that exude a sticky balm. Of course, the power went out and after the blow it took the men in our area five days to open a path for one car to the Athol line that was about three miles away. There were no chainsaws at that time, and we only had axes and two-man saws. We had luckily cut the timber on the right side of the flat and some on the left. Father had been counting on cutting a lot more in about a year. This would be a great loss in income. We didn't lose the barn. I think because of the barn framing it made it. A lot of barns in town were lost. I have been through several storms since but not anything as bad as that. It was two weeks before we had power. There is a mark on a service station in Athol showing the height of the water during the flood. It's ten feet up on the wall.

Three hundred yards down the road there is a bridge over the Millers River. Normally the water is eleven feet down from the bottom of that bridge. The date was September 21, 1938. Six hundred folks were killed in the New England states and there was three hundred and six million in property damage. Nature is not controllable by man which is why I don't believe we can control the supposed warming trend. If nature wants to get warmer she will in spite of man, not because.

We worked at the farm every year picking the buds from the new set out strawberry plants. Each year we set out the runners from the old beds to make new beds. Then, there were the plants that we sold by mail. We planted our new gardens in the spring and spent many hours weeding and hoeing around the seedlings. We planted all New England crops that would grow here. Potatoes--sweet corn--popcorn--radishes--lettuce--cabbage--cucumber--summer squash--carrots--winter squash--parsnips--melons--tomatoes--peas, a lot of peas as we sold them to the stores. A lot of folks from nearby towns would drive out into the country to buy from us in season. I sure used to hate hilling potatoes up. It was a lot of back breaking work until Dad bought a hiller to be horse drawn. That was a real help.

One thing about my Dad. He worked hard but he played too. Often on a real hot day around three o'clock he would say, "Let's go swimming." Ken and I were always ready. We would grab our suits and get in the old Buick and drive down to bottom of Davis Hill and down a cart path to the creek. The water was cold as hell but we loved it. We could swim almost as soon as we could walk. One place to swim was at the bottom of Davis Hill, the other was at the bottom of Doane's hill. Both were in the woods and we could drive to them on old cart paths. Dad loved to swim and Mom used to call him the walrus. He was about five ten and very big. He was the strongest man I ever knew. I once saw him lift the back end of a Model T Ford, that was stuck in the mud in front of the house. He was hard sometimes but he was a lot of fun too.

There was a place to swim on the way to Athol but you had to pay to use the water. It was called Packard Heights and old man Piquant owned the shore and made a living from it. He had set up picnic tables and charged for swimming. We didn't go there very often; the creeks were free. One year Mom made a deal for us to swim there all summer for a small set amount. It was great but, of course, we ruined it by being a big pain for the owner Mr.

Piquant. I don't think Dad ever went there at all, damned if he would pay to swim.

Ken and our friend Bob and I used to walk up Doane's Hill and back down through the woods to swim at Doane's Falls. What a great place to swim. In the middle of the falls at the top there is a hole about four feet deep that you can stand in. It's a wonderful feeling like a hot tub with the action of the water around you, only it wasn't warm it was ice cold. The falls were open to everyone, but we hardly ever saw anyone there, just us, so we always swam naked. Well this one hot day, Bob and I were in the pool but Ken was on the side. The Falls make a lot of noise and I thought I heard a giggle and looked up and there was a whole Girl Scout troop at the top of the falls all looking at Ken in all his glory. He couldn't hear them and didn't see them. We yelled at him to get into the water but he was trying to get his clothes on as he was cold. I looked up at the girls and they were laughing and having a great time at his expense. About then an older women showed up and put a stop to the fun. She marched them off, but I could see her grin. Well that was the last time we swam naked at the falls. We never heard anyone talk about this so I guess we didn't do any harm. We would never have admitted it had been us anyhow.

Every once and awhile Dad would decide to go horned pout fishing. We would take our old canoe which was a wide Canadian style and very stable. Sometimes our cousin Dan Shepardson would go with us. We would drive down an old cart path about a mile down the road from the house until we reached Long Pond. There was a camp where we stopped. I never saw anyone use that camp in my lifetime. It burned down years later. We would carry the canoe down a steep hill back of the camp, load it up at the landing, and paddle up the pond. Just below the pond there was a narrow place as you entered the start of the pond. Crossing in front of us, one time, was a big eight or ten-point buck with a doe following behind. That just added to the whole adventure.

Dad had his spots all marked. By looking at the shore he knew where we were. We would bait up and fish on the bottom. We would use handlines and would fill a big bucket with horned pout. They were not very big but fat as butter. Every once and awhile they would stop biting and Dad would say probably there was an eel around. Most of the time we would keep fishing, instead of moving, and sure enough one of us would catch an eel. We always brought an empty grain bag with us to hold the eel as they were slimy and hard to hold when you removed the hook. When it got dark we would light candles and set them on paddles laid across the canoe. Boy was it dark. You were in a little world consisting of only the boat. You couldn't see anything outside of the canoe. I loved it. Every once and awhile a winged hellgrammite would fly into the candle and you could see his nippers grab at the flame. In the larva form they made great bait for bass and such. In the winged stage, they looked fearsome, especially at night. One night we heard a bobcat yowl. It sent shivers down my back. Dad had shot several cats over the years. On my desk, I just looked up to see a picture of Dad all dressed up in a suit holding a big cat. He is holding it by the back feet even with his shoulders and its front feet come to the top of his shoes. That is the biggest cat (lynx rufus) I ever saw. We hardly ever see them in Massachusetts nowadays. When we pulled up our anchor and headed for shore as it was black as pitch, I never knew how Dad could find the landing, but he always did and within a few feet. The pout would still be alive in the morning and we would dress them for supper. They are hard to dress and we had to skin the eel and cut it up in pieces about three inches long. I never cared for eel but Mother and Dad loved it. Mother would roll the fish in corn meal and fry them. They were very good and we all ate them with a fine appetite. Those trips up to the pond night fishing will be with me forever.

Father loved to fish. He was an avid trout fisherman and loved to fly fish. At that time, not very many folks in the farm country fished fly. Mostly folks fished garden worms and night crawlers. Dad belonged to the elite fly fishing group. He was not ashamed to use worms but preferred flies. I used to go with him up to what we called the creek that ran into the head of Long Pond. In the spring, the mayfly would hatch and light on the water and the trout would grab them. Now they don't always hatch when one is there. So, you must be there at the right moment. The leader material that you tied your imitation fly to was not like today. They called it cat gut and you had to soften it in your mouth. I remember Dad on the way to the creek with a small roll of it in his mouth making it soft with saliva. This kind of fly fishing was called dry fly. You floated the fly on top of the water and set the hook when the trout grabbed it. It took a lot more skill then worm fishing.

I have a picture of Dad taken by Mrs. Putney up at Putney's Mill in Royalston. It's of Dad holding about an eighteen-inch native brook trout. You must remember they weren't stocking in those days. That was a great trout at any time. The bottom of the creek was covered with sawdust from a mill that had been on it maybe a hundred years ago. In the spring, we caught many a boatload of perch, pickerel, big suckers, horned pout, quivers, also called pumpkin seeds, dace, pond shiners and of course trout. Now days the trout are all stocked and browns and rainbows are in the mix. I took all my kids up that creek many times and they loved it as I did. I have three sons who love to fish. I also took my daughter fishing and she loved it. That's where two of my sons get their love of fishing. One son has a charter boat on Cape Cod and one runs a boat yard and charters. My oldest son also fishes when he can.

Dad had a reputation as a fisherman in the Athol Rod and Gun Club, and one Sunday, Dad and I stopped at the club to see how the fishing in the club pond was going. The club stocked the pond for members and you could fish it but you paid seventy-five cents for each fish if you kept it. When we got there, they were about twenty folks fishing and they wanted to have a contest to see who was the best fly fisherman. The idea was that all would put up two dollars and fish for an hour and the winner take all.

Two dollars was quite a bit of money for Dad but he almost had to put it up. He sent me for his rod from the car and tied on a May Fly as they were hatching in the sun. In about thirty minutes he was five fish ahead of anyone. God he was fast. If a fish grabbed it he was caught. Johnny Geradie was standing there and said, “Eri, let me see what you are using.” He caught the fly and Dad did not look at him and he took a pair of clippers and cut the hook off at the bend. I saw him do it but it really didn’t dawn on me what he did. Dad could not catch a fish after that and he got beat by one fish when the time ran out. He took it well and we walked back to the car and I told him I thought Johnny did something to his fly. Well he looked and found the hook cut off and said why didn’t I tell him? I felt terrible, I had let him down. Johnny ran a bar in Athol and the story got all over town and everyone got a big kick out of seeing Dad get beat. It wasn’t easy beating my father. The story goes that Dad walked into Johnny’s and everyone was kidding him about it. It must have seemed a little strange as everyone knew that Dad didn’t drink when he took it all with a smile and went over to the bar and told the bar tender to set up the house for a round of drinks. Everyone got their drinks except Dad and he told them to drink to Johnny as he was paying for them and left. Well that got all over town too.

As I am writing this I keep thinking about a lot of little things that Ken and I were taught that are not even thought to be important today. That is probably true but knowing some of those things will add an awful lot to your life. I tried to pass some of these things on to my children. What young man or woman today knows anything about wild flowers? We were taught to know their names and where to find them. Jack-in-the-pulpit, dog-tooth violet, Solomon's seal, painted large-flowered trilliums, mayflower, wild iris, blue-eyed grass, Dutchman's pipe, fringed gentian, cardinal flower, lady slipper and on and on. I heard you are not even supposed to pick mayflowers now days. Maybe because people pulled them up by the roots. When we were kids we were taught to always take scissors with us to cut mayflowers, never pull them up. I will admit I had more luck with my daughter learning than the boys. She always still asks me about how the trilliums look around our hunting camp. It adds so much to life if you know some of these flowers. Before every Memorial Day we all picked wild flowers to bring to school to decorate the soldiers' graves at the cemetery right below the school. We would all march, the whole school maybe forty kids, and place flowers on the graves. I also think it is a shame that very few folks can name but a few trees. Once and awhile I am surprised and meet a young man who does know a tree or two. It pleases me to see a spark of curiosity for that gives me hope! Well maybe it's only important to me.

When we were very young some folks by the name of Parker bought the old Tandy Place at the end of our road on the hill across what we called the main highway. They had two children, a girl named Grace and a boy named Raymond. They were too old for me but I remember them well, as they were friends of my sister Ena (NeNe) and my brother Don. I have been told that I named my Sister Ena NeNe because when I was little I could not say Ena so it came out NeNe. My nick name was Tuddy, most of the time shortened to Tud. For some reason, my sister named me that when I was two or so and it stuck with me. Even now some of my family still call me Tud. Raymond and Grace Parker were a lot of fun and I guess Don and NeNe liked them a lot.

Mother and Father were not ordinary people in any way. Dad was the worse tease that I ever knew. NeNe had been away from home quite a while and Dad used to drive her crazy at the table. She really got embarrassed, when she had a friend from nursing school come home with her. I remember one time when she was there and Grandpa Hager (Mom's dad) was there. Dad had been working, haying all morning and we were all having dinner. There was a platter of sweet corn for dinner and after about five ears or so Dad farted loudly. Sis was mortified. She told Dad it was disgraceful and sounded awful. Grandpa Hager grinned and said it just sounded corn-fed to him. Mother minded her own business and smiled. It really must have been awful for Sis. Sis could not let it go and kept bitching about it. She should have known better, it just encouraged Dad and he really didn't need any more encouragement. She was sitting across the table from Dad and he very calmly put a little butter on his table knife and buttered her nose. I knew what was going to happen as I had seen it before. Sis picked up her glass of water and threw it into Dad's face. That did it, water flew everywhere. Every once and a while this sort of thing was known to happen at our table. I don't remember Sis's friend's name, but I felt it was not right for her not to share in the fun, so I threw my water in her face. Well the water fight escalated and soon we were outdoors throwing buckets of water, running back and forth to the well for refills.

Sis was waiting around the corner to catch Dad with a bucket full when Raymond, from up the road, came around the corner and got the whole bucket. Well he was mad. Dad had told him he would take him to Athol to see his lady friend and he was all dressed up just so. Well that ended that water fight, one of many. I don't know when all this sort of thing started but it could happen almost any time. I don't know how Mother put up with it, but I saw her throw many a glass of water. I have wondered many times what Sis's friend thought of the whole thing. I do seem to remember her throwing water on Dad outside. I guess what Dad liked about it was it was so outrageous. It's only now that I realize what it must of seemed to visitors. My father had a great sense of humor, but country humor. I remember one time we had some distant relatives visiting from New York. When they arrived, it was easy to see they were out of their element. We had just butchered a pig and served it for supper when Mother's distant cousin remarked he could not find meat like this where they lived. Dad with a straight face said, "It's no wonder, this pork is not any of your murdered stuff. This pig we just found dead one morning." I don't remember the rest of the strained conversation after that. Well it was funny to me! I guess they took it alright as they came to see us many times over the years.

Dad had two boys that came to live with us. They were wards of the state and it was very common for some of the farms to take them on to help with the work. Both these boys were men grown by the time I was born and I only knew them as men. One was named Bill Gillis and I loved him like a brother. The other was Tom McDougal and I didn't like him at all. When he came to visit he always tried to straighten me out, as he put it. One thing for sure, he couldn't do it. He tried it once after Dad died when I was fourteen and I damn near decked him. I will never know as Mother stopped it. Bill on the other hand was a hunting buddy for years and years. He married a Royalston girl and lived in Athol all his life. He loved my Dad and thought of him as his own Dad who he had never known. He had quite a sense of humor and I remember one story that always stuck in my mind. Before I was born all our shotgun shells were loaded by hand with black powder. Dad had a friend called Bill Bucannon who hunted with him. The day before up at Long Pond the geese were flying too high to reach, and Bucannon figured he could load up and get a little more distance with his shot. Dad and Bill Gillis were sitting at the kitchen table loading shells for next Saturday's hunt. Bill said he wanted to load up some heavy loads and that he had some empty shells and could he load up from their powder and shot. Dad told him he could, but not to go over the heavy loads that were recommended. Well Bucannon told him he had a talk with an old market hunter and he had said you could put all you could get in the shell and it would not hurt anything at all. Dad said that you had to balance the load and it was foolish to try to better the recommended loads.

Well you couldn't tell Bill Bucannon anything. I know this to be true as I met him years later and we were soon arguing. As I write these words I can look at the wall in front of me and see a picture of Dad and Bill Bucannon just coming back from a hunt. Well the upshot of the story is that next Saturday they were all sitting in a bush blind in the canoe when Bucannon said, "Hear they come." They were coming all right, two gun shots high. Dad and Gillis pulled their heads down and there was a thunderous report and a yell of pain. The old double barrel had exploded the left barrel and taken off Bucannon's left thumb. They put a boot lace around it and paddled all the way down the pond to the landing where the car was and so to the hospital. They left him there and went back to get the canoe and take it home. In the bottom of the boat they found Bill's thumb. Gillis picked it up and put it in his pocket.

The next day he went to see poor old Bucannon and gave him a wrapped little box and when he opened it on a pillow of cotton lay his thumb. They say he got sick and Gillis was not too popular at the hospital from what I have been was told. The story went all around the hunting fraternity and sort of became a classic in hunting stories in the area. In the picture that I have you can see he is holding his cigar between his first two fingers and there is a marked lack of any thumb. The gun was destroyed and he went out and bought a gun that was not a good choice but you couldn't tell Bucannon anything. He bought a Winchester model 1911 semi auto. It kicked like hell and only a few were sold. There was a knurled section on the barrel so you could pump a shell into the chamber. It's a wonder someone wasn't killed when doing it. It kicked so bad it was called the "Headbuster."

When I was sixteen Bill Gillis and I shot a mink out of the car. We used bird shot but we still got sixteen dollars for it from Will Gerard. It was out of season so we were lucky to get anything. Will took off twenty-five cents a hole. On the wall at my brother Ken's house hangs Grandpa Luther's Double Barrel 1878 hammer shotgun. Ken and I are always amazed at the way he'd had it made just for him. He saved up his money to do this because no gun he tried was right for him. Talk about drop on a shotgun. Well when I shoulder it the barrels point almost at the ground. It must have something to do with his having only one leg. Mother told me that when he was walking he had to swing his wooden leg as there was no joint in it. I always wished I had known him.

When I was about four I remember my father used to run a trap line. The money from the fur was really needed for all of us. Hunting was a big part of our lives and trapping was just another part of the whole picture. One very cold morning he came in the back door with two big red foxes from his traps. They were dead and both stiff as a board from the cold. He laid them down on the kitchen floor in front of our built-in china cabinet on the back wall and sat down for breakfast. Ken and I were playing on the floor and crawled over to pet the foxes. Suddenly all hell broke loose. One of the foxes started to growl. Out from behind the stove came our old dog Pen. He grabbed the fox by the throat and threw it into the air, at the same time Dad jumped into the fray with a loaded club he always carried with him in a belt case when running the trap line. Holy smoke, I was scared out of my head. Dad, dog, fox, me all trying to get out of the way, Mother yelling, Ken crying and the fox dying. Whew what a mess. I can tell you Dad caught hell from Mother that morning. After they got the dog calmed down and Ken stopped crying, they started to laugh. It was good to hear. It was very reassuring. Later that day Dad went out to the barn and skinned out the foxes.

I remember several times when Dad came home with a mink, one time two of them. Boy was he happy about that. They were worth five times what a fox was worth and ten times a skunk. At about ten years of age I started to run a line but I never did well at it. The price of fur was way down for some reason and Dad had given it up, but he thought it would be good for me. I carried a little 410 single barrel shot gun on my rounds and got a rabbit once and awhile. We ate quite a few and I got sick of them, so after a while when one ran I just wouldn't see them. They were like squirrels, they were good the first few times but after a while one got so you hated the taste. One day I did get a shot at a bobcat but missed. That really hurt as the state paid a five-dollar bounty on them. I was a short-lived trapper but the experience always stayed with me. What we really liked to eat in the way of game was partridge, woodcock, pheasant and deer.

Times were hard and it was becoming very hard to make a living at farming. The farm was in Grammy's name and when she died it went to Dad. When she was alive there was no property tax from the town as she was a widow of a Civil War vet. After Grammy died Dad had to pay it. I can remember Mom and Dad talking about this being another expense. Dad got a small salary from the town, about three hundred a year as I remember. Over the years he served the town as Constable, Deputy Fire Warden, Fence Viewer, Town Moderator, Selectman and Assessor and served on the school committee for four years. Dad had gone to Mass. Agricultural College but had to give it up after a year as his Dad could not handle the farm. Luther got around very slow after his leg was amputated above the knee.

Dad also was a substitute mail carrier for the rural route in Royalston. He would fill in when the regular man was on vacation or sick. It was a welcome source of income when it happened. Ken or I used to ride with him now and then. Because of that we knew most everyone in the town. One time in the winter when Dad was delivering the mail, he stopped at the house for dinner and brought a box with him into the house. The temperature was about ten below and very windy. The box had a lot of slots in it and there was a baby alligator inside. You could look in thru the slots and see him. He was stiff as an old maid's skirt, so Dad had brought him in to warm up. After he was delivered I wonder how long he lived. They passed laws to stop that shipping of live pets. I never forgot how alive he looked after he warmed up. New England was not his cup of tea.

Royalston center had a general store and Post Office. I loved that little store, it had penny candy and once and awhile we would get some. The clerk was Millie French and she was like an institution there. Dad would stop there once and awhile and it was like a little center of the town.

Cliff Wilcox was the Postmaster and his father-in-law, who was called Frappy French, owned the business. Frappy took a trip to Athol every day in his Ford Model T truck to get supplies to sell in the store. That truck only went about twenty miles an hour and he would leave in the morning and get back late afternoon. I used to wonder if it could go any faster, but I rode back from Athol with him one time and it wouldn't. People used to say they set their clock by Frappy. I was told that he was a great character, but the trip I had with him one time was the most boring you could imagine. He used to be bundled up in a buffalo robe in the winter as the truck had no heat. The cab was wood and hardly kept the wind out. He was still taking that trip every day when I left elementary school. I wish I had that truck today.

Dad always stopped at the center store on the mail route to say hello. Most of the rural route was in what we called West Royalston. South Royalston had a general store and post office. South Royalston was the home of The American Woolen Mill. It employed one hundred and fifty men in 1916 but was destroyed by fire in 1933. South Royalston never really recovered from that disaster. At that time, the Millers River was starting to become polluted by the paper mills that dumped waste upstream. It was bad. When you went through South Royalston, it smelled so bad we used to hold our noses. Today it runs clean and full of fish again. It took about fifteen years and several court cases to get the Millers River cleaned up. When I was in my twenties I caught many a native brook trout in the small brooks that ran into the Millers

We shot quite a lot of deer. At that time farmers were allowed to shoot them if they were eating the gardens. After you killed a deer you called the Warden and he sent you a form to fill out and you kept the meat. You could not jacklight them at night, but during the day in the garden anything went. Dad loved guns as we all did. When you went out the back door and stood on the porch, you were looking out at what we called the flat. It was fields and gardens. It was about three hundred yards wide between two stone walls and was about fifteen hundred yards long. Now the deer were not too happy about coming into the close gardens as they seemed to lose a lot of their relatives in those areas. Now at the end of the flat was a big flat rock that stood up about three feet high and around four feet wide. My father decided that the only thing to do was to plant a lot of turnips and to move some raze berries down there. Maybe the deer would find it safer that far away. Well they did but it was a tough shot for the 30/30 and way too far for the shot gun. In 1914 before I was born, Savage Arms had come out with a Model 99 in 250/3000 which moved a 97-grain bullet at 3000 feet per second and was very accurate. Well the story goes Dad wanted it but he had to get Mother to agree. I don’t know how he did, but he must have as there was one in the gun cabinet. He had sighted it in with open sights by standing on the back porch and resting it on the clothesline strung between the posts. He had it so he could hit the big rock about three inches down and right in the middle. Ken and I used to walk down to the end of the flat just to admire the lead splashes on the rock. One of my sons, Eric, has this rifle today. It killed a lot of deer. I'll bet Dad was the only man in the whole area, maybe in the state, to own a 250/3000. He used to talk about that rifle at the feed store with the other local men.

It worked very well, he could lay them low even at that long distance. Most of the deer he killed at that range were shot before I was born, but I can remember Mother giving me a knife and telling me to run down the flat as she could see he had one down. She always said, "Hold the knife with the blade out and away from your body when you run." We ate a lot of deer meat. The farm was a place for Dad's friends to gather for bird hunts. He was well known in the area and had a lot of friends. My oldest brother Don would almost always be there as one of the party. Along with Bill Gillis, Bun Coffin, Red Anderson, Bill Buchanan, minus thumb, and several others. Several of the men had pointers or setters. We always had a hunting dog. The first I remember was Old Penny who we called Pen, he of fox killing fame. He was a German short haired pointer. He died before I hunted and we got a finely bred pointer who was worthless. Dad got rid of that dog, gave it to a friend as a pet, and got a beautiful brown and white setter. One of the small breeds, a Llewellin. That dog was by Dad's admission the best he ever had. We called him Dickie. He trained so fast and easy it was hard to believe. He retrieved at once and loved every second of it. When we started to put him on grouse he started to point right off and if you spoke softly to him he would hold his point till you were ready. He hunted close and loved us all. Some dogs don't like woodcock and won't retrieve them. Not Dickie, he was the best. My Dad always said that every man should have at least one really good dog and a good woman in his life. Well he did and so did I. I hunted Dickie all thru my high school years and even after I got home from the Marines, after World War Two. It was a sad day when I had to put him down. We always put our own dogs down. It just seems right somehow. It would have been too impersonal for me to leave him at the vet's. There is a bond between hunters and their dogs that unless you have been there you would not understand. I don't know why I feel so defensive about it. Maybe because by today's standards it seems barbaric. Now days we let others do the unpleasant if we can.

All of the Stewarts used side by side guns for grouse and the same for deer. Rifles were not allowed in Massachusetts for hunting deer. We only used the rifle for out of season deer. The new rifled slug had come out and was a big improvement. I killed my first five deer with a twenty-gauge shotgun. Once I got two, seconds apart. At that time there was quite a lot of grouse, biddys we called them. I can remember seeing Dad and several of his friends in the backyard laying out birds between the porch posts that were about twelve feet apart. It was a great sight to me. There would be ten or so grouse, a woodcock or four, four or five pheasants and they would damn near go from post to post. Dad used a Lefever 20-gauge double with fitted side plates. My brother Ken has that gun today. He has had it all done over and it is a little beauty. I remember when Dad got that gun. One day a car came skidding into the backyard and Fred Wood, who lived below the Shepardsons, jumped out. There was a hole in the roof over the backseat and he was upset. It seems he had been losing some of his chickens to a fox and kept his gun handy. That morning he saw him down the road in the lower field and jumped into his car to drive down to get a shot. He jumped out of the car and slipped the safe off, but the fox took off before he could shoot. In disgust, he opened the back door and tossed the gun in the back and of course it went off right through the roof. Dad tried to explain why he thought it happened, but Fred wanted no part of that gun. He said he would never trust it again and asked Dad if he wanted it. Dad said how much and if I remember right, he said give me twenty dollars and it's yours. He bought it and it never went off on him. He used that gun the rest of his life. Ken and I always remembered that whole episode and treated that gun very carefully. I killed a lot of birds with that gun. The new shells used to feather at the ends when fired. I think the chambers were for shorter shells then we were using at the time. When it was done over the gunsmith said it was chambered for two and a half inch shells and he corrected it. God it's a wonder we didn't get hurt with it. Dad even used it for shooting trap once and awhile. I don't think it was two and a half inch chambers. I just think the crimps on the new shells we were using made them longer when we fired them. I compared them with the old fired shells and they were three sixteenths longer. I think the gunsmith just relieved the chambers a little. It did not kick as much after it was redone.

There were a few run-ins with the Game Warden. Well, that was bound to happen sooner or later. Most of the time there was no problem. One day Dad and my brother Don were hunting off the old Gulf Road with the dog (Dickey) when they met a young man that they knew only slightly and he invited himself to go along with them. This is a big no-no in hunting circles. You never ask to shoot birds over another man's dog unless invited. For some reason, Dad didn't say a word. I can't imagine my brother not telling him to hit the road but he didn't. Well Dickey went on point and put up three birds but before the young man knew what was going on, Dad shot two and Don got one and the dog retrieved them. He was so out classed it was pitiful. He didn't get the message and continued behind them. The dog went on point and a partridge flushed. At the same time a hen pheasant flushed. They were illegal and Dad shot the partridge. At the same time the young man fired. The dog went out and brought back a hen pheasant. Dad turned to give the kid hell and saw him walking off through the brush. They knew the Warden was in the area so Dad told Don to hide it in the stone wall. They sent out the dog and he came back after hunting for five minutes with the partridge. They hunted the rest of the day and went home where he told us all about it. Around ten o'clock the next day the Warden, Arthur Lovely, came to see Dad and wrote him a ticket for shooting a hen pheasant. He had the bird with him. Dad told him the story but he decided to take Dad to court. He did and lied on the stand by saying he saw Dad shoot the hen. We all knew what had happened. The kid whose nose was out of joint because Dad and Don wouldn't give him a shot must have shot it and then saw Don hide it in the wall and told Arthur that Dad shot it. Even today I find it hard to believe that the judge who knew Dad would believe that story. It was all over town and all his friends got a big kick out of it. Dad lost his Hunting and Fishing license for a year. That was a long year.

A lot of my memories are of things that happened that I was told about. One was about my brother Don's first deer hunting trip. It seems that he was not supposed to hunt for another year as he still had a year to go before he was old enough by law. Father said that the law allowed him to hunt on our own land at any age as far as he was concerned, and he was right. Dad and Bill Gillis, Bun Coffin and Red Anderson were all going to hunt the farm that day. So, Don got his old Hunter Arms double that Dad had given him and off they went. In those days, we almost always had snow opening day and that day was no different. Don told me that there was about three inches. They took Don up an old cart path to the corner of the old stone wall by the old foundation of the Metcalf place. It was near the swamp where we picked blueberries every year. Dad told Don to stand by a low spot in the wall where very often when startled the deer crossed. About eleven o'clock he heard something coming and it sounded like it was really moving. He was loaded with what we called round ball or pumpkin ball. Over the wall came a big buck and Don dropped it. He started to run over to it when a doe jumped over the wall. He dropped her too. Well about thirty minutes later when Dad and Red Anderson got there, Don was walking about a foot off the ground. They gutted them and dragged the two deer back to the farm and hung them in the barn. It was about two o'clock and they decided to make one more small push in what we called the Mill Yard. They told Don they would see him at supper and took off. Well Don's blood was up and he couldn't sit still so he told Mother he was going to sit out near the Mill Yard wall just in case one came that way. He stood by the old wall in sight of the house and promptly shot another doe. Don thought that was easy but it was about ten years before he shot another. After that he shot many but only one at a time.

Almost all the town was open to hunting at that time. The land that wasn't we all knew and steered clear. Everyone knew Mrs. Delange would take a shot at you if she caught you on her land. Well at least she was open about it. Now Crazy Brown, as he was called by the deer hunters, was a little different matter. His farm was the only one on a road which was a mile or so in the woods. His problem was that he thought he owned the whole road and he didn't. At the end of the road was his farm and he owned about three hundred acres, but most of the land going along the road to his house was owned by someone else. So, if you were parked on the road as it was town road he couldn't stop you. He just was not a happy man. God, I don't know why. His wife Fanny was about Mother's age and damned good looking. Fanny seemed to have a thing for Dad. Once a year the Grange held a dance at Town Hall and Mom said Fanny was always after Dad to dance. Now Crazy Brown never came to dances that I ever saw. He just wasn't sociable.

Year after year we use to hear stories about his run-ins with the hunters. He met Don and his best friend Bob Bridges hunting near his land and showed them his pistol and told Don he would shoot him if he didn't get out of there in one minute. Bob, standing with his loaded shot gun, calmly spit his chaw on the ground and inquired what Mr. Brown thought he would be doing in that minute. Well that was the end of that encounter. Crazy got very frustrated over the years and I guess the boys just wore him down. Opening day 1939 he cracked and lost it. We all knew something was bound to happen. I remember reading about it in the paper. Just as daylight came on opening day, Crazy walked down the road and took the gas cap off the first car and peed in the gas tank. He had enough left for another and proceeded to administer his vengeance. Folks always thought that he went home to refill his tank as he got three more before he got caught. It seems one of the young hunters had not been feeling well that morning and had been sleeping in one of the cars that Crazy was servicing. Imagine the surprise when he stepped out and caught Crazy with weapon in hand and discharging. That little episode cost Mr. Brown a lot of money and gave the town a great story for quite a while. With an eyewitness, he had to pay for five cars. We never knew how much but I'll bet his wife was unhappy. "Vengeance is mine sayeth the Lord," not yours Mr. Brown.

I was up to the home place last summer and on the way, I decided to go by Grandpa Hager's place just to see how it looked after all these years. It looked fine and I decided to cut over to the Old Keene Road and come out on the main highway toward the farm. The road used to go all the way through before the Tully Dam was built, so I went to the end of the road just to see how it looked as I had not done that for years. At the very end, there was an old wood weather-worn chair sitting under a big oak tree. I wondered if the chair had been placed there by a hunter hoping for a deer to come by. It looked like a damn good place for one to come by. For some reason, I felt I just had to go over and sit in that chair. Well I did and found out it had been used by a hunter. When I got up to leave I turned to go back to my car and in the crotch of a branch in the big oak tree I saw two shotgun shells. I looked at them and found they were slugs so I had found the answer to the chair in the woods.

I got into my car and turned around to come back to take the turn onto the main road, and when I went by Jessie Willis's place I started to grin thinking of Jessie. Jessie never married as far as I knew. She had a friend who was blind and lived about three miles from her. Joe Macman lived by himself when I was young in a little house with a barn about three times the size of his house. Jessie was his friend. He had been born blind and got around amazingly well. I used to see him working in his garden. Jessie was what we called a handsome woman and was her own person and in no uncertain terms. She did beautiful drawings in pen and ink and was very talented. She owned her own farm and ran it herself. I think it had been her father's place and she had inherited it. The reason I grinned as I went by was I was thinking of one day Dad and I were going by her place and she waved us to stop. She had been mowing by hand and was in a pair of blue overalls. When she got over to the car I noticed that she had no shirt on and was sort of hanging out on both sides of the bib. Well it didn't bother her at all and it didn't seem to bother Dad either so I pretended it didn't bother me. I found it kind of fascinating. It was sort of like boob peek-a-boo. When she came over she blew her nose on the way. She just closed one side at a time with her finger and let it rip. That made for a rather startling shift in positions but I manfully took it in stride. We moved on down the road and I sneaked a look at Dad. He never said a work but I do remember him telling Mother about Jessie mowing. What a great joy it was to know folks like Jessie.

I had no money. At least none to speak of. I complained to Dad and he came up with an idea that sounded great to me. I was eleven at the time and knew almost everything there was to know, I thought. It was a wonder I could keep my hat on my big head. The idea was that Dad would get me a dozen young laying hens and I would raise them, and he and Mother would buy them from me for the table along with the eggs. He would advance the money for grain and for the purchase price of the hens. We had one empty hen house at the time and I would use that. It seemed great to me and I could hardly wait for the hens to arrive. I had no idea of using any of my hens for dinner. They would lay their little hearts out for me and the eggs would soon put me on easy street. I think Ken was a little jealous, little did he know. Well they arrived. I went down the first morning to get a basketful of eggs. I got one egg but Dad said they would settle down in a couple of days. He presented me with the bill and I was in debt for the first time. Well they didn't lay worth a damn but got a little better over time. I used to talk to them as I fed them and told them if they didn't do better they would end up in the pot. It didn't seem to impress them at all.

Well, to make matters worse, one morning I found one of my hens very pale and dead. I called Dad and he said a weasel had killed it. He said it had to get into the coop and to make sure that there were no holes for them to get in. It was summer and I had plenty of time, so I went over that coop for hours. They were starting to lay much better and I could see my way out of debt. Three days later I went to get my eggs and found two more of my hens stretched out dead. Well that did it. It was war. Dad said I would have to get that weasel or he would get all the hens one by one. That night I got my 410-shot gun and stayed all night in the house with my hens. I kept falling asleep but nothing happened. The next night I was very sleepy and fell asleep very soon. Suddenly, I was awake, something was upsetting the hens. They were clucking and making all kinds of noise. I looked down the perch and here came a weasel. Without even thinking I raised my gun and blew him and two hens away. Well that was the end of my endeavor. I only had six hens left and they wouldn't even get me out of the hole. So, I sold out at a loss, it cost my Dad but he seemed to think it worth it.

I think I will add a little farm humor, nonsense, doggerel, whatever. My dear Mother use to say this. Cranberry pie and apple sass. The old man died with a rag in his ass. The rag blew out, the breath blew in and the old man lived and breathed again. I never heard that anywhere but from Mother or Dad. Now isn't that a great claim to fame? Country humor—name the three principal parts of a wood stove that everyone should know. Lifter, Leg and Poker.

Mother and Dad were not just farmers. They were much more. They were both past Masters of The Grange and had many things that they did to make life interesting. Mother painted and all of us have pictures that she painted over the years. I have four and one very large one she did when she was quite young. That has always been a bone of contention between Ken and me. It is a picture of two deer in a valley between two mountains. One of the deer has a repaired hole in its side. When we were about seven and five, Mother had fallen and injured her leg. It had not healed properly and gave trouble the rest of her life. She was in bed very sick and we were playing in the living room. I had a pop gun that I could shoot a marble out of and Ken had a bow and arrow that shot arrows with a hard rubber tip. I think I shot the deer with the pop gun. Ken is sure that he shot it with the arrow. We both think we are right. Dad saw it and went in and told Mom that we shot her deer. He was not too upset but Mother was, she cried.

Mother sewed all the time, she made many clothes for us. Most of the kids at that time wore handmade a lot. Most of our store-bought clothes came from Sears and Roebuck. I wore what was called riding britches and lace up high leather boots most of the time. On the right boot at the outside top was a little case with a snap cover to carry your jackknife. We all carried jackknives. That was part of being a boy or man. I guess we weren't as violent as today or maybe we considered a knife a tool instead of a weapon. I wish we still thought that way today. The boots were not waterproof and had to be treated with a grease, that we called dubbing. They had to be treated every couple of weeks in the wet weather. I thought they looked splendid. A lot of us wore aviator helmets with ear flaps that buttoned under your chin. You know, like Charles Lindberg or Amelia Earhart, our heroes. Almost all of us wore flannel shirts and long underwear in the winter. For a while when I first started school, knickers were being worn. I hated them like I hated Ovaltine. Of course, if you drank that, you could send the label in and get a little Orphan Annie decoder badge. You could send secret messages to your best friend at school. That was quite a fad for a time till our teacher Miss Elliott got a badge of her own. I don't think she ever used it. One day it just showed up on her desk and that was the end of all secret messages.

Mother and Dad were into photography. Before I was born they had taken many pictures and developed them. Many were in sepia and some were blue. As kids, these fascinated us as it showed our brother and sister before we were born. It was almost as though we were two different families. After my sister was born it was eleven years before I was born. It meant that my older brother and sister knew Mom and Dad at a different age and time.

When they were young, Dad was into taxidermy. Ken and I always loved the big horned owl he had mounted. There was a seagull that he had shot on long pond and mounted. It was very rare at that time to see a gull so far inland. Today they may be anywhere in the state. Of course, there was a deer head mount. He had the whole course and I use to read how to do it and wonder if I could. He had courses on all kinds of things. Dad and Mom were into all sorts endeavors. About 1937 Dad bought out a man that had a Raleigh franchise. This was a business that was door to door sales. This and another such business called Watson's were very big in rural areas. As kids, we always loved to see these salesmen come around. They always had a stick of gum for us kids. The man Dad bought out was a friend and he had a route where Dad knew most everyone. It was aimed for the farm folks that got to town only once and awhile, and Dad was very good at it, but he was too easy with credit. He had a 1934 Buick business coup and it had a trunk that could open right through into the back. There were two little jump seats in the back so he could still get us all into it at one time. When he started this business, Ken and I tried to help out with the milking and some of the farm work. We stopped selling strawberry plants by mail as Dad could not do it all. Around 1939 I remember Mother saying that he was grossing around one hundred dollars a week. I never knew how much of it was profit but that was not too bad for then.

Dad had volunteered to raise pheasants for the Athol Rod and Gun Club. They wanted to raise three hundred a year and release them just before the season opened. One spring in 1933 about ten men from the club arrived at the farm with lumber and rolls of chicken wire. They built three big pens covered with wire, walls and ceilings, with one door. Two weeks later a big truck arrived with boxes of young pheasants. The club bought bags of food, turkey pellets for us to feed them. We installed water containers and we were ready. Ken and I did a lot of the feeding and liked to see them strut around. Most of the birds were cocks. We had some hens mixed in but neither sex lived over the winter very well. They were never able to increase the population enough to pay. The winters were just too tough. Each year the club sent up some of the members to catch them and take them all over Royalston and Athol to release them for hunting. They always put quite a few out on our property as it was always open for anyone to hunt. The state of Massachusetts also released birds each year. Well the novelty of having the pheasant's pens in the orchard wore off soon.

About this time, Ken and I had discovered bean blowers and the fun of shooting with them. They were sold in the store for one penny and we got damn good with them. Ken was deadly with his. We got so we could sit empty shot gun shells on the fence and drop back about ten feet and knock them off most every shot. The biggest problem was finding small rocks to fit right. We didn't have any dried beans available. We tried the turkey pellets and low and behold they were just perfect. They were about a half inch long and made a real tight fit in the barrel. One end was fitted with a wooden mouth piece, and if you loaded it with a turkey pellet and gave a good blow, it would really move. We tried it out on each other a few times but gave that up as it hurt too much. One afternoon we were out by the pheasant pens watching the almost fully grown big cocks walk around. Ken loaded up and rested the shooter thru the fence on the wire and blew. He hit a big cock pheasant in the head and almost knocked him over. Of course, I tried it too and soon we hit seven or eight. We were having a great time but suddenly, we noticed there were several birds that we had hit that were having a hard time walking a straight line. In fact, they were staggering around sort of in a circle. We thought it was funny but felt a little uneasy so slowed down a little.

I was about to shoot another one when Ken said he could see Dad coming back from Athol. We felt a little nervous and ran back to the house to greet him. Supper was almost ready and we went in to wash up. For some reason Dad decided to walk out to see how the birds looked. When he came in we all set down for supper and Dad said he couldn't figure what was the matter with the birds. Several of them were walking in circles like they were drunk. Ken and I didn't even look up, just kept eating. I didn't dare look at him. Mother and Dad mentioned it several times at supper and Dad went out to check on them later. Ken and I were really worried and tried to stay as quiet as possible. He came back in and said they seemed fine but he had never seen anything like that before. We worried about it for a few days but the birds seemed fine. We never told Father. I don't think he would have found it funny.

Dad had hired a man to work for us on the farm. He was with us for about four years. He was paid twenty dollars a month and board. He was not too bright but knew how to work. Once and awhile he would drink but not around Dad. I never saw my Father take a drink. My Mother would take one now and then when she was around sixty. Forest was our hired man's name. A couple of years ago my brother Ken and I were laughing about the time Forest took our cow up to Peterson's to be bred. He had to walk him up all the way to Pete's, wait and then walk him home. Hell, it was at least six miles one way. Well the day wore on and Ken and I kept wondering when he was coming back. Around five o'clock in the afternoon he arrived. The cow looked fine but Forest a little looped. We ran down to the barn to see him and he greeted us saying, "If you never seed a man what's drunk you've seed one now." I don't know how he managed to sober up before supper but he did. I only saw my Father angry one time and that was the day he fired Forest.

Melons were hard to grow. Our season was not long enough usually, but this year we got them in early and they didn't freeze in the spring. Dad was watching them all the time and one day in early September he said to Forest before he left for work, "Make sure you cover the melons tonight, I think it may freeze." They were almost ready to pick, a couple of days more and they were ours. At supper that night he asked Forest again if he had covered the melons and Forest assured him he had. Dad was up early the next morning and we were having breakfast when he came in and said, "I thought I told you to cover the melons." "I did," said Forest. Father reached across the table and literally picked Forest out of the chair and pushed him out the kitchen door and pointed him toward the garden. Forest kept trying to say something, but every time he opened his mouth he was shoved forward. I had never seen Dad so angry. He got to the garden and said, "Do you call those covered?" All Forest had done was pull them together and throw the vines over them. They were frozen. Father told him to get his gear together and that he was fired, no man that worked for him could lie to him. When the school bus came for us Forest got on, suitcase and all. The other kids on the bus just looked but it was very quiet all the way. He could walk home from the school. I'll tell you the truth, my Dad scared me that day. Mother never said a word.

After Forest was fired we had another man. Arthur Talbut was his name. He worked days and went home at night. He cut fire wood for the winter for us and Dad wanted him to stay on. He lived in West Royalston with his wife Christine Brewer, in a little tarpaper covered shack. They had just married and I remember him showing Mother how his new wife had sewed up his jacket after it was ripped. She told him that his wife had a lot of talent and that he was lucky to marry so fine a seamstress. That's one of the ways young women were judged in town. Well we couldn't keep him, he had a chance to hire on at The Quabbin project for big money. In 1936, they were moving 7,561 bodies that were buried in 34 cemeteries, to a new cemetery in Belchertown, Mass. They had to be moved to make way for the reservoir that would eradicate four towns. The towns that were destroyed were Dana, Enfield, Greenwich and Prescott. The whole area was empty by 1939 and the reservoir was filled by 1946. About 2,500 persons in 650 homes were compelled to relocate. Well it was hard work and not for the faint of heart, but the pay was good and he had to go. He was the only man I ever knew at that time that used a double bitted axe.

Mother's dad, Arthur Hager, had a brother Otis that ran a dry goods store and post office in Dana. Mother and I went down to see him the day before he closed. He stamped an envelope, for Mother with the last post mark of the office and destroyed the stamp. Mother kept it for the rest of her life. Everything had to go and all was 75% off. Mother bought shoes for Ken and I and whatever she could afford. The town was almost empty and I had a very sad feeling. Fires had been burning for months. The smell of that and the somber mood of everyone stayed with me for days. At least it gave jobs to a lot of men who were out of work. They came from all over the country to find work there, but a lot of folks lost their homes and a way of life never to be replaced for them. I was only around nine and yet that whole Quabbin time stays with me to this day. It meant to me that nothing is permanent or secure and everything changes sooner or later. What the hell, we all have to grow up and smell the manure along with the roses.

Some time, along about 1935, we had two men disappear. One lived down along the main road to Athol, his name was Luke Thompson. He was about 82 and very independent. Well one day come supper, no one could find him. His grandson and a neighbor, Fred Woods, looked till dark. Next morning the call for help went out. Well neighbors looked all day and with no result except they found a wheelbarrow in the woods back of the house. His folks said that he had a habit of going out and picking up kindling wood for the wood box. That night they called the town constable Alger, and he said they would organize a search. They all met the next morning in Thompson's yard and started a hunt. Sometime in the early evening he was found almost where they found the wheel barrow two days before. My brother Don had found the barrow and felt bad that he had not spent more time in the area that day. The doctor said it wouldn't have made any difference when he was found and that he had died from a heart attack right off.

About two months later another man just disappeared. He was not all that old. Dad told me he was only sixty but nobody had seen him for the last three days. This time a Boy Scout troop from Athol came to help and half the town turned out. They used to meet at the farm in the morning and search all day in the surrounding woods. He lived in a little house that he built at the top of Davis Hill. I can only remember his first name, Arnold. He was a very nice man but no one seemed to know his life's history. The men went to his house and found that he had taken his hunting rifle with him. They also found that he had left his watch and chain under his pillow. Mother said she was sure that he intended to commit suicide. She said when time is no longer important to a man it means for him, it's over. After many days, the folks gave up the hunt.

This took place in August, and in the spring the following year, Mr. Fry went down the hill through the woods to his camp on Long Pond. He and his wife opened the camp and decided, as it was a warm spring day, to take a walk up toward the head of the pond. About ten minutes later, walking along in the marsh grass they saw something glitter in the light and went over and found the remains of Arnold. He had been shot through the side of his head probably by the gun with him, but that gun was not the gun that was missing from his home. No one ever found the gun that everyone thought Mr. Arnold had taken with him. At the time Mr. Fry was the town Constable and thought it should be investigated.

Well he tried but couldn't even find where the gun he was found with came from. Nothing ever came of the enquiry that was held and we all wondered what really happened. We never found out.

About 1934 the old Tandy place at the end of our road was purchased by Captain and Maria Ospinsky from New York. He had been a Captain in the Russian navy and that's the only name I ever knew him by. He was a mathematician for an insurance firm. He was very stern and quiet as far as Ken and I were concerned. Now Maria, she was something different. We soon learned to call her Madam. She liked to be called that and we loved to. We very seldom saw the Captain. Madam came up in the spring and stayed into the early fall every year. She loved the old place. It had a fireplace in every room as it used to be a tavern in the eighteen hundreds. Up the woods behind the house there was a spring house, not in very good repair, but the water was wonderful. The water from that was fed by gravity all the way down to the Shepardson barn and kitchen sink. It was kept running, a little all winter so that it would not freeze up. Just up behind the old house Ken and I had found the remains of an old stagecoach. We took Madam to see it and she was thrilled. In the Tandy house, there was no central heat that I remember. There was a well that was run by an electric pump and the house had two real bathrooms. The second summer Madam lived there her two johns and her sinks backed up and she hired a plumber. He told her she would have to have a new cesspool dug. She hired me and I dug a hole in the front lawn six feet across and six feet deep. I got Ken to help me and we put in about four feet of crushed stone that she bought from a mason who had some left over from a driveway he had installed for Fred Woods. The plumber came and installed the waste lines, we filled it in and as far as I know it still works today. Boy that was a big hole for a thirteen-year-old boy to dig.

Madam and Mother became great friends. She was about Mother's age, maybe a little younger, around forty-four I think. She put on outrageous clothes for Royalston. She would have very short shorts and a cloth halter and I think that was all. She was the talk of the neighborhood. She used to come down to the house once and awhile to use Mother's sewing machine. I remember one time we were having dinner and Dad didn't know she was in the other room sewing, and Mother asked him if he was going to drive into Athol and that Madam wanted to go in with him. She did not have a car. Well Dad said he hoped that she would put on some better clothes then she usually wore. He didn't want to be seen with her in those damn shorts. From the other room came a voice loudly, "I HEARD THAT." Dad was a little upset that Mother forgot to tell him that Madam could hear him. He really thought the world of her but he'd be damned if he would take her downtown dressed like that. Well she put on a dress and he took her. Every morning either Ken or I would walk up to the end of the road and bring her a quart of

milk. Imagine that right out of the cow. You couldn't sell milk right out of the cow today. It would have to be pasteurized. Ken and I had tried some of that pasteurized milk at Aunt Sadie's last Thanksgiving and found it disgusting.

We did a lot of work for Madam. We weeded her garden and cleaned out the wall by the front. It gave us a chance to earn a little money. I'll never forget one morning we were weeding by her stone wall and she was helping. I saw Ken looking kind of funny and I look up and low and behold one of Madam's boobs was hanging out. About then she noticed us looking and very calmly tucked it back in and went right on. Well Ken and I thought it was funny and damn near died trying to keep a straight face. She was a great friend for several years. We all loved her.

Many years later Sis went to visit her in New York and said she was just the same as we remembered her. I think she spent summers in Royalston for about seven years. She was a great comfort to Mother when Dad died.

Luke Shepardson was Grammy's brother and of course Dad's uncle. Luke had two sons, John and Carl. Carl had three sons, one of them was Dan who spent the summers at Shepardson farm. Dan Shepardson was eight years older then I. I thought that the sun rose and set on him. Whenever we could we were up on the hill in the woods across from the Shepardson's farm shooting squirrels and whatever. I don't think either one of us ever told anybody what we did one late afternoon. Dan was given some time off from his chores and we were up on the hill shooting his 22. Luke was down in the barn milking and from where we were on the hill we could see the barn and the cow stable. It was a still day and we could hear Luke talking to the cow to move over and hold still. Well about then a big squirrel jumped in a tree in front of us and without even thinking I shot. A split second later we heard the cow give a bellow and from what we learned later kicked over the milk pail. Well I can tell you we knew what we had done. You notice I said we. I damn sure wasn't going to take all the blame. Everything seemed to be quiet after a while and we sneaked down off the hill. Uncle Luke told Dan at breakfast the next morning that he couldn't figure what was the matter with the old cow as she was usually calm but something had got into her. He said she had kicked over the milk pail and it had been almost full.

Dan did not enlighten him. I worried most of the night and I am sure Dan did too. The next morning, I went over to see Dan and he said come into the barn, I want to show you something. We went into the cow stall and looked at the cow and sure enough there was a very small hole high up on her rear. You could hardly see it but if you felt it you could feel the bullet just under the skin. My God we were sure lucky. We could have hit Uncle Luke. We got away with it, the cow was fine and never kicked over the pail again. We never shot toward the barn again. Dan married and lived in Athol for a big share of his life with his wife Mickey. They are two of the finest folks I've ever known.

Our horse rake was old and it was beyond repair and Dad found one over in Tully Village. He told me one morning to ride Jerry over the old road to Tully Village and hook it up and bring it home. That damn rake was about twelve feet wide and I had to come home through what we called the narrows. Coming home by the old dirt road I had to cross the pond. The road being just a narrow little dirt road that split it in two, the rake was wider than the road. Well one wheel or the other would have to be in the water all the way across. I couldn't go any other way as I would be on the highway with traffic and the rake was too wide. I told Dad I was nervous about the narrows. What if I met a car? Well sure enough about half way across my worst fears were met. Not only that, but this guy was in a hurry and he expected me to get out of his way. I was about half way to the end when we met and he yelled at me to turn around and give him passage. Well hell I couldn't turn around, the water was too deep. I just sat there and let him run down until he gave up and backed up. He wanted to know who I was and said he was going to see my father and straighten him out. I sure would like to have seen that. Believe me, that would have been a very short meet. Boy I sure was glad to drive into the backyard at home.

That was the same summer that we helped with the haying at Shepardson's. They had about twenty-five acres to hay and not all flat like ours. Their team mowed and we had good weather, so it went very smooth for the most part. Then disaster struck. I was running the horse rake and raking scatterings while the others were loading up the hay wagon. I had just finished and had tied up our horse, old Jerry, to an apple tree to rest in the shade. I went to get a drink of water and when I got back I saw that the side of the tree was covered with blood. Jerry was bleeding out of his nose. I ran to get Dad and we unhitched him and I slowly walked him back to the barn. Dad called the vet. But he died in about an hour. Now I know this may not seem to you as a great catastrophe but to us it was really a problem. Not only had we lost a work horse who had given us many years of faithful service but he was part of the family. He was a great horse, gentle, smart and very strong.

That night at supper we all were very quiet. Ken and I just listened to Mom and Dad try to figure out what to do about replacing him. In the past when we had to replace a horse, we always bought an old one that we knew had been treated well. This time Dad thought maybe we should go to some other idea. Dad's friend Percy Chace had been trying to get Dad to take an old twenty-eight Buick that we owned and put a low geared rear end in it and make a tractor out of it. A good horse would cost about a hundred and fifty dollars and he thought we could get the tractor set up for about half that price. Dad called Percy and he said he knew where he could get a proper rear end geared down for us for thirty dollars and he would do the work for twenty dollars. Well if it worked out and if we could plow with it we would be way ahead. Percy came up two weekends and put together the best damn homemade tractor I ever saw. We got many years out of it. It had two draw backs, it took two men to work it and it had no breaks. One man to drive and one man to run the plow or mowing machine. The damn thing wouldn't stop when it hit an obstacle like a horse would and we broke several plow points. Running the mowing machine with the tractor with one of us in the seat and guiding the cutter over rocks and such was dangerous as hell.

After Dad died, Ken and I had some pretty bad arguments over the whole thing when we mowed in our teens. If you didn't lift the cutter blade fast enough over a rock and it caught, you couldn't stop the tractor, like a horse. A horse would feel the catch and stop immediately and no damage, but if you were running the tractor you couldn't throw it out of gear fast enough. If you were sitting on the mowing machine you were in a seat fixed to a big piece of spring steel so that you would ride comfortable.

What would happen was when the cutter bar caught, the machine would twist toward the cutter bar on the right. The spring seat would compress and it would throw you about eight feet off the machine and on the ground ahead of the cutter bar. Being the oldest I would be on the mowing machine and it would hurt and scare the hell out of me, and of course I would yell at Ken and blame him for almost killing me. It wasn't his fault but I gave him hell. He almost quit several times but I wouldn't let him. Those haying days were not the best for us. Things like that I don't think my brother ever forgave me for, or maybe me just being two years older is what he resented. I think he still does to this day. I always wanted to ask him but it's too late now. As I write this I'm ninety-one years old. Today is Saturday, the twentieth day of May, 2017. My brother Kenneth died at the age of 88 the thirtieth day of January, 2017. I will miss him forever.

I find myself thinking about Percy and Ruth Chase. I think of the many nights they spent with Mother and Dad playing cards. Contract Bridge was becoming for some the only game in town. Aunty brought it home to us and we all played. Ken and I played in our teens and for the rest of our lives. Dad and Mother loved it and played with several couples.

Aunty taught Ken and I for the most part. My sister who lived to 97 played as often as she could and was one of the best players I ever knew. To play with her when she was in her nineties was remarkable. Another game that was sweeping the country was called Monopoly. Ken and I loved it. It was really a great game for making friends, but maybe not for keeping them. Mom and Dad played many a game with Percy and Ruth but Percy and Dad ganged up on the two ladies and all hell broke loose. One night Mother and Ruth exploded. Ken and I were in bed but we got the repercussions the next few days. I don't think Mother spoke to Father for two or three days. In her entire life, eighty-six years, she never played the game again. In the winter, there were many times when we would be snowed in for a week or ten days waiting for the plow to come by. Ken and I would become very restless and get cabin fever. We would try to get Mother to play Monopoly with us but it was just a waste of time. When Mother made up her mind it was like trying to close the barn door against the wind, but with less success. I don't remember Dad ever mentioning the whole episode. I guess he knew better.

When we got snowed in, I mean really in, four or five feet on the level and more where it drifted, you just had to wait until the town tractor came by. You could hear it coming from quite a way off. It was a caterpillar with a V blade and sometimes would be in front of the house fifteen minutes or so to get the drifts open. When they were done there was a path one car wide and if you met anyone you had to back up to the nearest open spot to pass. They would make one now and then. Now when you came to Doan's Hill all bets were off. If you made it, fine, but if you didn't or met a car and had to back down, it was pure hell.

The only thing that saved me from going mad in snowed in times was books. I read everything I could get my hands on. *Tom Sawyer, Huckleberry Finn*, Zane Grey's books and one I remember called *Dick Onslow Among the Indians*. I heard Mother and Dad and my sister, who was home on one of her visits, talking about a book called *Tobacco Road*, and got the idea she gave a copy to Mom and Dad. It sounded naughty. A few days after she left I tried to find it. I finally found it under their pillow and of course read it. I liked it but never told them I had found it. I also read *Gone with the Wind* and it became my favorite for many years. My folks never tried to censor my reading at any time that I can remember. We could not afford any magazines except The Saturday Evening Post, but we had friends that took other magazines and saved them for us. We got McCall's, Life, and Look. They were great and I read them from end to end. Sometimes they were a month late or so but it didn't hurt them at all for me. In Look, I saw pictures and read about things that I just couldn't understand. Black folks that had been beaten and hung. Pictures of Bonnie and Clyde shot to pieces. The KKK marching down the street for the hate of Black folks. Well I thought maybe I would understand when I grew up, but I grew up and I didn't. Even so, the love of literature has stayed with me all my life. I can't imagine life without books.

In 1933 when I was seven years old, my brother Don got married to Evelyn Phinney who lived in Orange, Massachusetts. Can you believe it? We were flower boys and marched down the aisle first, dropping flowers along the way. It was the first wedding Ken and I had ever been to and we were quite impressed and I felt rather silly, but Mother was smiling and I didn't dare look at Dad. Don went to work for S. W. Cards in Mansfield Mass. They made taps and dies. He was a very talented machinist and head of the lathe room for many years. Don and I, years later, built a hunting camp and spent many years hunting together. Most of the time we got along pretty well. I never cared about getting a deer as much as he did. I just liked to be in the woods and enjoy the fun we had at camp. My sons love it too. We get together every year to hunt and play cards at camp. Well, we used to, but at my age now it would be too damn hard.

As you are growing up you have no idea what the future holds. That is, as the kids say today, not a bad thing. That my wife Elizabeth and I would spend twenty years living beside my sister and Marguerite, my cousin, would have been at that time unbelievable. Aunty My, as all my kids called her, was like a second sister to me. I can't remember when she and Sis were not a part of my life. We lost Aunty My ten years ago. She lived back in the woods next door in a house I had built for her and her husband Howie who died before she did. I ended up being the last one here. As Ken and I were growing up, our cousin My was at the farm with Sis a lot and her boyfriend Howard Hastings (Howie) used to come to pick her up for dates. As kids we liked him but made his life as miserable as possible. If you were dating our cousin or sister that was our duty. Well we all lived together for many years on Cape Cod. For some reason, my sister and I were always very close. Ken never shared that but by his own choice. I never understood why. After George, my sister's husband, died Sis moved in with her son Tim and his wife Pricilla in Athol, Massachusetts. My's brother Russell use to come up to the farm to help with the haying and Ken and I were very fond of him.

Now I come to Dad's sister Aunt Ena. We called her Aunty. She was a teacher and taught bookkeeping at the high school in Gardner, Massachusetts. She loved to read and gave me my love of books. She gave me books for Christmas, for birthdays, for holidays, for snow days, for good school marks, for fun. I read them all. When Ken and I were quite young, Aunty and Grammy both read to us. In Grammy's case it would be from the Bible. Aunty lived in Gardner where she taught. She was the one that made sure all her nephews and nieces had good dental care. At that time teeth did not last very long. Most older folks I knew had lost their teeth long ago. Folks just didn't go for dental care as we do today. Once a year we would be checked at school and you could have work done at town hall, but it wasn't free and a lot of folks would turn it down. I never knew my Dad when he didn't have false teeth. Most of Mother's were false too. I thought everybody had had false teeth as they got older. Aunty had excellent teeth and saw no reason why we shouldn't. She bought us tooth brushes and insisted we use them. She insisted on paying for our dental care. I was lucky as I never had a cavity till I went in the Marine Corp at eighteen. All of us nieces and nephews will always be grateful for Aunty's help. Aunty had a steady job so she would buy a new car every three years. She always bought a Chevy. As kids, we could hardly wait to see Aunty's new car and get her to take us for a ride and maybe, if we were lucky, get her to buy us an ice cream cone. There was a little drug store in Athol called Vittman's and they sold FORJOY ice cream. I guess that brand name is long gone. When I get an ice cream cone, even today, that name FORJOY always comes to mind. It so describes the way we felt back in depression times when we had a treat. Just think, you could get an ice cream cone for five cents and a double for a dime. Not only that but the cones were square and there was a square dipper to match. When I got home from World War Two, the square cones seemed to be gone. Aunty died in 1975 at the age of ninety-five. I will always miss her. After Dad's death, Mom and Aunty lived together over thirty years. How many sister-in-laws do you know who could even spend a year together?

Christmas at the farm was a great day for Ken and me but nerve wracking. Mother's sister, Aunt Edith, along with her husband Alfred Brown, with our three cousins Roger, Jean and Eleanor along with Gramper Hager always came. Now Aunt Edith was about as slow and unorganized as a Mason leading a Knights of Columbus parade. Eleanor was Sis's age and taught school and did not always come, as often she would be invited somewhere else with friends. Then there was Jean, who died very young and Roger, who was younger than Ken.

Aunt Edith had married a Royalston man, Alfred Brown, who was not a fast-moving man either. Dinner would always be set for one o'clock and Edith never was on time and it used to drive us all crazy. Now I mean late, sometimes as late as three or four, and when they arrived they would act as if they were just a little late. I never could understand why we just didn't go ahead and start without them but we never did, and Father never seemed to be upset at all. Everything was cooked on a big wood burning stove and when it was ready it was not all that easy to just keep it warm and it drove Mother to distraction. Sis was there and once and a while Don and of course Aunty, but it was sort of the family joke about when Uncle Al and Aunt Edith would arrive. Well they eventually would, but by then we kids would have worried holes in most of the paper on our presents so we knew what we were getting. Mother would keep calling them and they were always just getting into the car according to Uncle Al. Well it was stressful but a great day and lasted longer than planned because we started so late. One year it got to be five o-clock and there was no answer when Mom called them. Don said something must have happened, maybe their car broke down. He and Dad got into the car and headed for Athol. When they came over the hill just before Damon River they could see a car sort of tipped and caught on a stump just this side of the bridge. Later Dad told us he could see Uncle Alfred standing by the fender as if waiting for help. When they got there Al said no one was hurt and he had lost control of the car because of the ice. He said he thought they were going to go right through the bridge rail but luckily, they tipped up, went through and caught on that big stump. They all got together and tipped the car back off the stump and onto the road. He shook Dad's hand and again said no one had been hurt and that he was hungry. The car started right up and Don took Aunt Edith and Jean and headed for home. Dad said he would drive so he took Uncle Al and Roger in their car and followed. That no one was hurt was sort of like a Christmas Miracle.

Dad and Mom loved Christmas and tried on a very small income to give us a great day. We cut our own tree on our own land every year and some of the decorations I remember were from Dad's childhood. There were even some tin holders for candles. When Mother and Dad were children, Mom told us they were placed on the branches and the candles were lighted. I guess it was beautiful but it must have been dangerous. We always had ribbon candy at Christmas. No one seems to have it now days, for some reason it lost its popularity over the years. I wonder why? Well maybe time changes everything, even the candy.

Now Thanksgiving was a little different. For Thanksgiving, we went to Aunt Sadie's and Uncle Watson's. Now Dad's sister Aunt Sadie was not disorganized at all. She was married to Watson Amasa Hall. They also lived in Athol where Watson had his own room which was very big with a cot in the corner by a big double hung window. When we were very young he had a battery radio, later on it was electric. Ken and I always thought it was strange that he had his own room but never spoke of it. Everyone knew "HE DRANK." As kids, we really liked him. He could play the ocarina, the banjo, the piccolo, and the Jews Harp. We liked him a lot but realized he was not paid very much attention too. "HE DRANK" a great deal. I never remember him and Aunt Sadie even having a conversation of more than a few words.

One thing Ken and I liked at Aunt Sadie's was the flush toilet. It was fascinating to say the least. We could hardly wait to use it. There was a big oak box on the wall three feet above the seat and when you pulled the handle there was a rush of water and everything was carried down the hole. We used to wonder where it ended up. Neither one of us asked, it didn't seem the thing to do. Aunt Sadie had a big black stove that looked like ours but it ran on gas. She lived in a three-story narrow house with hardly any room between her house and her neighbors. Years later after the house was torn down I went by trying to show my children where Aunty My use to live, and I could hardly believe the small space the house had been crammed into.

We would have a wonderful meal with everything any one could want in the way of extras. There was no wine or any type of alcoholic drink. Not just because of Watson as my Father and Mother did not drink at all. It was a real great day and after dinner we would sit at the table and Ken and I would listen to the wisdom of the older generation. Uncle Watson would go back to his room. He never looked upset over being ignored, after all, "HE DRANK." That house was always very clean and very tidy. All the woodwork was hard southern yellow pine and finished with clear varnish. The whole house had a shiny look inside. Believe it or not, that house had a hallway, seven rooms and a bath. In the front of the house there was a small porch that seemed scary to Ken and me as it was up three stories. Mother told us to stay off the porch but we use to sneak out on it till we were missed.

Athol was a very quiet little town, but it seemed like an exciting large metropolis to Ken and me. I don't remember the date but sometime in the late thirties everything started to go wrong in Aunt Sadie's life. Uncle Watson seemed to be drinking more than ever, and no one could figure where he got the money. One Saturday morning the police arrived with a warrant and, when searching Uncle Watson's room, found seven Starrett Micrometers under his mattress. The police said Watson had been under surveillance for a long time. He had been stealing parts from his bench where he assembled and checked them for accuracy. He had been caught selling them to a small machine shop in Worcester.

He was arrested, fired and stood trial and allowed to pay restitution rather than serve time. Of course, the whole town knew and it must have been hard for Aunt Sadie and our cousins Russell and My.

Years later Ken and I were talking about those times, and he said he always wondered if Aunty helped them out. Now it got even worse. Aunt Sadie had been giving piano lessons for years, but after Watson had been arrested she lost almost half of her pupils. She took a full-time job in the Athol Cotton Factory. With Watson not working she was the bread winner alone. That winter was very cold and we had a lot of snow. It got dark very early and one night Aunt Sadie was walking home and had to cross the street in front of her house. She stepped into the street and a car that was going too fast saw her and put on the breaks, skidded, and hit her. Dad told us she was dragged under the car ten yards at least. She was in the hospital six weeks and I will always remember she had marks on her face when she came out of the hospital that remained for the rest of her life. My and Russell were both married but helped out and Aunt Sadie got through it. As far as I know, Watson never had another job in his life. Why she ever stayed with him I'll never know. Ken said to me one time, "Maybe she still loved him."

I remember one Thanksgiving when we got home there was the remains of what had been a mouse on the back porch. We all wondered what had killed it. Every now and then in the morning, when one of us went out to the woodshed to use the outhouse, you would find another part of a mouse laying there. The remains were always in about the same place. Every winter Dad would open the screen door back against the wall as it was not needed till spring. The little bits of mice were usually in front of that door. Time and time again we would put on the light to try and see what was catching a mouse, but to no avail. One night Dad went out and happened to look up at the screen door and sitting on the top was a little saw-whet owl. He didn't move and Dad figured he was sort of blinded by the light. Ken and I wanted to catch him and teased Dad to help us but he was not very enthusiastic about it. Well that little owl was there almost every night and we finally got Dad to show some interest. He took a fish net and put it over him just as easy as pie. Oops, now we had an owl. What do you do after you've caught one?

Mother had a large covered tin bread box and we punched holes in it to let the air in and put him in. We would open the cover and there he was. He didn't seem upset at all and would snap his beak with a loud snap and turn his head all the way around and spin it back. I didn't know an owl could do that and I was totally fascinated by this and had hopes of making a pet of him. That was not to be. What do you feed an owl? As far as I could see he ate mice. Well we caught one and offered it to him. He wouldn't even look at it, just kept snapping his beak and turning his head around in what I thought was pure disgust. Mother and Dad never said a word. I think they knew that we would come to the right decision. I held on as long as I could but he wouldn't eat. I kept thinking of the skunk that we'd had when I was very small. Mother had remover his scent gland which always remained a mystery to me and he was a great pet for quite a while.

Oh my, to be the only kid with an owl. I could just see myself going to school with him perched on my shoulder. Well he wouldn't eat and one night we all said good bye and I set him back on the top of the door and went inside and put out the light. I always thought he liked me, after all he let me put him back on the door without making a fuss but the next morning he was gone and we never saw him again. I don't think he wanted that experience repeated. Well there went my dreams of being different, I guess I was doomed to be just me. That's always worked best for me anyhow.

That winter, after our owl episode, Mother and Dad decided to have a sugaring off party. I guess I will have to explain what that is as most folks today wouldn't know. Every year we tapped the sugar maples and boiled the sap down in the sugar house that was up behind the Tandy place. We shared the house with the Shepardsons and both families made maple syrup there. You tap the trees, collect the sap and boil it down, and what's left after straining out the dirt, bugs and such is maple syrup. Using our trees, it took about 45 gallons of sap to produce one gallon of syrup. The sap was poured into shallow long pans and set over wood fires that we kept burning day and night until the season was done. Some springs the season was short and the yield poor. You never knew how it would be. It had to freeze at night and thaw every day to make the sap run. Don told me Dad didn't go at it as hard as he used to before I was born. It was now more a relaxed endeavor. We'd had a pretty good run the year before or maybe it was just time for a party.

As far as I can remember this would be my first sugaring off event. About twenty folks arrived from the neighborhood and some from Athol. I think this was about 1936. They all got there and Mother had asked them to bring milk pans, at least the ones that had cows. You took the pans and filled them with snow packed full and tamped down hard. On the stove were pans of maple syrup that would be heated till the syrup was thick. Then you brought the snow-filled pans over to the stove and the ladies would take a spoonful and trickle it on the snow. Then you would wind it up on a fork and put it in your mouth. It turned into the most delicious candy you will ever have in your life. Kind of chewy and then the sweetest taste imaginable.

On top of that we served cider. You had to be careful not to over indulge. There was no liquor, I don't know if any of the folks drank liquor, but the Shepardsons and the Stewarts did not and did not serve it either. Well to me it was really great. There were not many kids but my favorite cousin Danny Shepardson was there, and I hung around him and listened to everybody talk. Of course, before the evening was over I had to sing. At that time, I was singing Harry Lauder's songs. Father had always sung them and I guess I was supposed to keep the tradition up. Dad was in a lot of Black Face Minstrel shows that the town put on for Royalston Day every year. You couldn't do that today. We would be accused of racism. Dad was great on the stage and had a fine singing voice. I never knew it was not the right thing to do until years later it was explained to me by the enlightened folks of the world. I still wonder if not knowing made it wrong. Oh well, my philosophy of life is mine and does not necessarily run in the same bumpy path as the enlightened. Mine has very few bumps. For once we stayed up until the party was over. I think it was around ten thirty when folks started to leave.

It was at this party that I heard several funny stories about folks I had known all my life, ones that lasted down through the years. There was one told about Uncle Luke and Aunt Nellie, not in their presences however. It seemed that Uncle Luke would come to breakfast every morning and sit down to the table and with studied deliberation dump the entire cream pitcher on his oatmeal, whereupon Aunt Nellie would say, “Why Luke that’s cream.” Luke would grin and say, “Spoilt it, ain’t I?” Things between man and wife, what a joy.

Another story that was told is about Warren Sherwood when he was about six. I’ll bet he got some sick of hearing it as he got older. It seemed his Grandpa Sherwood had saved his money and bought an Edison Victrola. Little Warren was the apple of his Grandpa's eye and he showed him how to wind it and play it. One day Grampa Sherwood said to Warren, "Now Warren when I die this Victrola will be yours." Warren quick as a wink came back with "Grandpa, do you think it will be before spring?"

Dan Shepardson was very slow speaking and had a droll sense of humor. He was not a great church goer and was not fond of the new Baptist preacher in West Royalston. He went to church there in the summer because he was living at the Shepardson farm and that's where the family went to church. Dan was very stubborn and got into an argument with the preacher over the church picnic about the time it was to be held. It was to be held in the middle of haying season and Dan thought it would be easier to have it after the hay was in and maybe it would be a little cooler. Dan thought it was very petty of the preacher not to see his point of view. He was told that the date was set and that was that. The next Sunday Dan embarrassed the whole family at church. It seems the preacher's sermon was on how it was that the little things in life were the most important, and he tried to prove it from the Bible. I was told by folks that were there that it was pretty boring and everyone was glad when it was over. As the congregation left out through the door the preacher was standing at the exit shaking hands and such. When Dan and the family came through he shook hands with Uncle Luke and Aunt Nellie and asked them how they liked the sermon. They said it was just fine and the preacher asked Dan how he enjoyed the truths as he preached. Well, Dan said in a loud, clear slow voice, "I guess little things please little minds," and kept walking out. Luke was mortified. Knowing Dan as I do, I have always loved that story and just wished that I had been there.

Mother thought Ken and I should go to Sunday school and tried to get us to agree but it was not a great success. I don't remember Dad going to church and Mother only went once and a while. The Baptist Church closed in town and she started to take us to Athol to the Congregational Church. I did very well as I had been brought up on Bible verses with Grammy Stewart. Well they thought I was so good that they decided to put me in an older class and that was a mistake. I lost interest right off and was bored to death. After that I hated it at any level. Well one cold Sunday morning Mother got us ready to go to Sunday school. It was a hell of a job as we fought Mother about getting dressed up and getting our hair combed. She didn't seem to get much help from Dad about our behavior. He was sitting in the living room by the stove reading the Saturday Evening Post and made very little comment. Father was never very much help about getting us ready for any trip. She finally got us ready and we got into the car. We had no heater and it was cold as hell so we got a blanket over our legs and our feet got cold as usual and off we went.

Inside of two minutes the windshield was covered with ice and you could hardly see out at all. The only thing we had to help with the ice was a little fan mounted on the steering post but it took a long time for it to make a little hole to see out of. That fan was a little killer. It was just open with hard rubber blades and every once and a while you would hit it with your fingers and it hurt. I think the car was a 1928 Buick four door. It was sort of like a covered wagon with attitude. On the posts between the front and back door there were little holders where you could put flowers if you wanted to. It was glare ice on the roads and Mother was trying to be very careful and we kids were fussing and out from under the blankets. Mother was telling us to sit down and behave. We were just going by the piggery about four miles from the house when the car started to skid. I was standing by the back door and grabbed the handle and the door swung open and out I went. I hung on that handle like there was no tomorrow. The car turned three hundred and sixty degrees and headed for home. The door swung shut with me still on it. Mother looked to see if I had made it back in and never said a word. She just went home. I don't remember what she said to Dad when we got home. I was just glad to get home. That was the last time I remember going to Sunday School. Maybe that was a message from above.

When Grammy Stewart was alive so was religion in our lives. No cards, no dancing around, just Bible verses, prayer and quiet. My sister and my older brother Don tell about how it was for them when they were young. They told Ken and I that when Dad took the family to church he would sit in the car and read while they all went to church. They could never figure out how he got away with such behavior with his mother there. In those days, there was a traveling preacher who came around in the rural areas. He was still doing it when I was very young but I really don't remember it very well. He would always come in the late afternoon as part of the deal was that at each house he would get supper and a bed for the night. He came about once a month. In our case it was a combined visit with us and the Shepardsons.

He held what was called a prayer meeting after supper. He would preach the gospel according to him and then you all set around until the sprit moved you to speak. They said the sprit never seemed to move Dad. Now this preacher's name was the Reverend Trefeatherin and he was as bald as mount Monadnock, not even a fringe from the neck up. Don told us that when the sprit seemed to move Aunt Nellie she always said the same thing, never changing even one word. It was always "Lord may your will be done."

Now this particular evening after she spoke, it didn't seem to move anyone else so the Reverend decided to close with his usual prayer. He had a chair in front of him to rest his elbows on as he performed. You were judged by your performance. He kneeled and started to get ready to thunder his words but there was a problem. Aunty Nellie's cat who had been minding her own business had to be moved out of the way as she had climbed on the chair. Perhaps the sprit had moved her. The Reverend picked him up rather forcefully and proceeded to go on. The candle light was shining on the Reverend's bald head and it was just too much for Aunt Nellie's cat. She got up on her hind legs and sort of kneaded his shiny bald head. The cat got him damn good and he tried to brush him off, but to no avail. Don and Sis were dying trying not to laugh, and one way or another it scared away any spirits that were left over. Well Aunt Nellie put some iodine on the Reverend's scalp and that was the end of the evening. I must have heard that story four or five times over the years. My sister says that I was there but I was very little and probably slept through the whole thing.

As I think of these stories I wonder if they are only funny to me. Maybe you have to understand how uncomplicated our everyday life was compared with today. No income tax, no social security, no television, no PTA, and no damn texting, on and on. Of course, you could make the same argument in reverse. I must say that I don't remember any one ever being in therapy. If you weren't right you just stayed that way and everyone put up with you. Well we are so much smarter today. Today we spend all kinds of money to make ourselves right but folks still have to put up with us. Every one of us hears the wind howling at a different pitch.

There were quite a few families in town that needed a helping hand now and then. One such family was the Brewers. They lived in West Royalston. I used to go by their house when I took the horse up to Ed Hamlet's to his blacksmith shop to get shod. I would get on old Jerry and ride him up the road. It was about five miles one way and I really liked the ride. There were usually two or three men at the shop talking, and it was a real treat for me to listen to what was going on in the west part of town. This was around 1933 when they still had their own school in West Royalston. One time a lady by the name of Linny Durant stopped in with her riding horse for new shoes. She had never been married and kept house for her dad, Walter Durant, after her mother died. She probably was around forty and every available man in town had tried to arouse her interest. Even some who were only available in their minds. If she had been alive today I think she would have agreed with Gloria Steinem who said, "A woman needs a man like a fish needs a bicycle."

Now Linny was not against hunting, she enjoyed deer meat and usually got a deer ever year. I guess her problem was her totally unpredictable thought process. Four years ago, a hunter had wounded a young buck behind Walter Durant's and it had run into the barn through the open door. Linny had forgotten to close it after milking that morning. I guess she must have felt sorry for him so she closed the door and kept him. No one will ever know how she did it but she took care of him, healed his gunshot wound and for the next four years she had a shadow. Whenever she was out he was beside her. He grew magnificent eight-point horns and one morning he was gone. The next deer season we all expected someone would get him but no one ever did as far as anyone knows. There used to be a story going around town that once and awhile Linny would take a basket of apples and leave them for him at some secluded spot. I don't know if it was true or not but Ken and I just loved her.

There was also a Baptist Church for this small community that we went to once and I while, so of course I recognized most everyone. It was great fun to be at the Blacksmiths. Well to get back to the Brewers reminds me of another story my mother told me. Dad and Hollis Chace decided that they both needed meat and they knew that Buck Whittfield had been having a lot of trouble with deer coming into his garden at night, so they thought they would help him out and remove a couple. Of course, it wasn't legal, you had to own the land yourself, but the deer didn't know. It was a slow night and they didn't have any luck until about one in the morning when a big doe decided to try the turnips. Hollis shot him and they field dressed her and put her in the back of

Hollis's car and started for home.

They got almost to the Brewers when Dad said he could smell smoke. They went around the bend in the road and found the Brewer house in flames. Mom said that they didn't even discuss it, just stopped the car and ran for the house. No one was out of the house and it was roaring. They rushed a side door which caved in easily. The whole house was just a big tarpaper covered shack. Dad told Mom the smoke was awful and they had to grab the kids and both parents out of bed as they were overcome by the smoke. Let me tell you that was a big job. I don't know how many as all were not born then. Dad and Hollis got them all out and everyone recovered. The doctor told them afterwards that a few minutes later and most of them would have been dead. Our one fire truck got there but of course it was too late to save anything. Dad and Hollis were getting a little nervous with what was in the car and wanted to leave. Both of them were burned and it was very painful and they wanted to leave before someone asked what they were doing at two in the morning so far from home. Well they got away finally and headed home. We heard later that the town was going to nominate them for a medal for heroism. Dad and Hollis put a stop to that in a hurry.

They wouldn't even talk to the papers. They didn't want any questions asked about that night.

The town got together with the Red Cross and built the Brewers the best home they had ever owned. Ken and I went to school with four of the Brewers, two boys and two girls. The kids were named using the alphabet. The story in town was that they went as far as M for Markus, but his Mother said he had a head shaped like a sugar loaf and she thought they wouldn't push their luck. That may be true but I think there might have been another reason. Right after Marcus was born the town hired a new school teacher for the West Royalston School and I guess she was cute but showed poor judgment. There had been talk of combining the West Royalston School with the center school and it was finally decided as, low and behold, the new teacher ran off with the Brewer's daddy. Good old Lester. I use to wonder if Mrs. Brewer missed him or heaved a sigh of relief.

The town was stunned but it made up their minds about combining the two schools. That's how we ended up with the combined total of pupils. We kids at the center were kind of worried about so many new faces but it worked out fine. The romantic couple left town and I never heard about them again, but there were remarks about this romance for many a week. The only thing Ken or I ever heard about them was when one day at the store we heard Mille French tell Clift Wilcox she had heard they were living up in Maine. It was very hard on the children. At school the other kids didn't know what to say, so for once they kept quiet. The three Brewer children, in school, were very cautious around us but I for one felt very sympathetic toward them. I just couldn't imagine what they must have been feeling.

That part of town, West Royalston, was like South Royalston except South Royalston kept its own school. They each had a little community center. West Royalston even had a library in the Baptist Church that was open for all. It was sad but the whole church was dying. The congregation got smaller and smaller and the society just let it go. It was really a sin. The library for the time was fantastic. I almost cried when I was hunting up that way in the early fifties to see that it was falling down. Ken was with me and we went into what was left of the library and saw that the books were mouse eaten and soaking wet. I picked up a first edition of The Wizard of Oz, all hand colored and completely ruined. That would be worth about three hundred today if you could even find one. The Church and Library belonged to the Baptist Society. My mother, who had been Baptist, at one time wrote them, but they just let it go. A lot of rare books were lost in this debacle. The church burned down and shortly after that I was told that the Baptist Society came out and picked up the bell.

Our Blacksmith Ed Hamlet had three sons Clive, Roger and Sherman. They all married and stayed in town. Sherman was the last to be married and he found himself a widow gal, Julia, who came from city life. I guess it was a bit of a cultural shock for her to move out into rural life. Sherman was a carpenter and went up on the Butterworth Road and built his new bride a house. At that time, the road was about five miles long with three houses counting his. She had a daughter that was one year older then I was. She seemed quite polished and refined to me. I thought like sugar, I really liked her. I don't think she even knew I was alive. All the girls thought she was wonderful. As far as folks knew, everything was fine, but there was trouble in paradise as often happens when cultures clash. Julia was not happy going from an oil-fired furnace to a wood stove. The story goes that Julia wanted to move back to what she was used to. Who can blame her? Well Sherman wouldn't move. So, the tale started. He came home one night and found his wife in tears and scared to death. It seemed she had been attacked by some sort of a mad man. She had got away and got into the house and got Sherman's rifle and took a shot at him as he was trying to break in through the window. She claimed that he had broken the window and that she thought she hit him. Well Sherman looked outside and found blood and called the State Police. They called the town constable and he called Dad to let him know there was a wild man on the loose. Well Dad went up. The State Police had dogs and were all set to go on a man hunt. Dad looked the situation over and told them that he didn't believe the whole story.

He found big pieces of glass outside and felt that if this man broke the window from the outside, that the big pieces would be inside. Well most of them believed Julia but it didn't look right to Dad. They all went into the woods to see if they could follow the blood trail. It ended on the ledge up back of the house and Dad said, why don't you let the dog loose? They did and after a while heard him yip and yip again, and over the ledge he come with a mouth full of quills. They grabbed the dog to get out the quills and Dad went up over the ledge and found a fresh porcupine that had been shot and cut open. That was where the blood had come from. Julia had shot it and opened it and dragged it as if someone had left a blood trail. Well she was caught and Dad went home. He said he thought it was all baloney. He said that he thought she didn't like living out in the woods and he figured she'd probably leave Sherman. He was wrong as they stayed married all their lives but moved to a different house on a tar road about two miles away.

While I was in the Marines in World War Two, our woodshed started to fall down. As it held our outhouse, something had to be done. Mother hired Sherman Hamlet to build a new woodshed and outhouse. Ken helped him most of one summer and it turned out fine. Ken told me he got to know Sherman and really liked him.

About fifteen years ago I was going up to my hunting camp in Sandy Hollow in Royalston. I came in from South Royalston and turned to go down the hill by Roger Chase's and found the house had burned down. Roger had died seven years ago and I started to think about him as I drove on to camp. Both he and his brothers, Elliot and Hollis, had been folks that I had known all my life. Roger was a real old-time sort of guy. I remember one time when Don and I were coming back from hunting deer in New Hampshire. As we passed Roger's house, Don made a remark that the old timers were few and far between now days. As we passed the barn we could see a light on the roof. We slowed down to see clearer and be damned if it wasn't Roger on the roof fixing a leak with new shingles. The light was a lantern and the roof was steep but it had to be done so he did it. Devotion to life and to responsibility.

About four years before that I had stopped in at Royalston Day and talked to Roger, he was seventy-two at the time and had been a widower for ten years. He said to me "I just don't understand these women in town, there they are all alone and I can't seem to get them interested in me at all. Why it's a shame, why just last year I won the hundred-yard dash right here with all these young fellows against me. I just don't know what they could possibly want that I can't furnish. Why just this morning I baked two blueberry pies and they're sitting on the kitchen table cooling." Well I didn't know what to say to that, so I wished him luck and told him he looked fine. He did too.

Roger had been married to his wife, Elmina, for forty years. Everyone in town knew everyone else and if any one told anything out of class it got around sooner or later. I don't pretend to know how this got out, but I suspect Elmina told some one of her friends at Grange. Well one spring Elmina wanted to visit with her sister in Warwick, New Hampshire and she wanted to go for two weeks. Roger would have none of that. He said he just could not be alone for that length of time. Why he would just go mad. Well she said if he would let her go, that when she got back she would give him all the sex he wanted for a month. He thought it over and decided that it sounded like a pretty good deal. So, he agrees and Roger drove her up to Warwick and drove back home alone. I don't know about him but she said she had a wonderful time with her sister. From what I always heard, Roger planted more in the garden that spring than ever before. He stayed real busy those two weeks.

Elmina came home and, like all good Baptist women, she kept her promise. The very first week Roger had to go to the doctor with a sprained back, now I mean sprained. He was in bed for three days. Poor Roger, sometimes when fortune rises it floods. Well I can tell you the whole town loved that story. I always wondered if he knew that. When I was about fourteen I heard the story for the first time. Most folks just can't help telling everything they hear.

Two summers later Roger and Elmina wanted to buy a different car. Their Model A needed a lot of work and they saw an ad for a car in a Gardner dealership in the paper that sounded good. They went to Gardner and tried to make the deal but they couldn't make it to their satisfaction so came home. The salesman was Percy Brown and he'd be damned if he was going to lose this deal. Two or three days later Percy took the car home with him and stopped at Roger's to see if he could sweeten up the deal a little and make the sale. He knocked on the farmhouse front door and, getting no response, went around to the back door. No one answered so when he turned to leave he could see their old car down at the end of the field. He knew there was a brook down there and figured maybe they were having supper at the brook. He walked down the field and down a short path and he thought he heard a horse whiney. He figured well that's the story, they are taking the horse down for a drink, so he came right on. Oh my, there was Elmina like- September Morn- but bent over standing in the brook and well mounted by Roger who would let out a whiney every now and then. Percy backed up the path but just couldn't bring himself to turn around until he was out of sight. He just couldn't take his eyes off that woodland frolic. Now he should have kept his mouth shut but of course he didn't. My brother Ken worked as a mechanic for that dealership and he told Ken the next morning and of course Ken told me. As you can see, my description is as told to me. I talked to Percy and I think it's about right. I admire Elmina and Roger as I firmly believe it is the finest hot day activity I know of. What a wonderful flavor to life it adds to be privileged to know people that make life an adventure.

As I write this, my thoughts go back to what else makes life an adventure. In the sixties, I went to camp a lot and went to my favorite places in the world, to fish the little brooks that still had native trout. Most of these places were in Royalston. One of the most beautiful was the Newton Brook. I would stop in South Royalston and park at the site where the old woolen mill used to stand. There is only a big tall chimney left. The site is beside the Miller's River and very desolate. I would park and load up for a long hike. It would be in the spring around May or early June as that was the best time to fish the Newton Brook. Later in the summer, the brook would not have many trout. The level would go down and the brook would run just a small trickle with only a pool or two to fish. It was the early fishing I wanted. Now brook fishing is becoming hard to find in Massachusetts as most of the brooks that are still running do not have a population of trout. I am talking about the little brooks. I don't think very many folks fish those anymore and haven't for years. For this kind of fishing you take a light rod, a can for worms, and a creel to hold the trout and you're off. You should be prepared to be gone three or four hours at least if you are going with me. I am on the right side of the river facing downstream and off I go. I walk down stream along the river. It's about eight in the morning and it's going to be hot. The black flies are just waking up and realizing that food is coming along the bank. I hate them but it's worth it.

This particular morning it's bright blue and smells of spring. The bank is covered with loose stones as the river overflows every year and removes the top soil leaving a great path for twisting an ankle. I am wearing old sneakers and no socks as I expect to get wet. Most of the trees along the banks are well budded and a lot are in full bloom. There's a splash and three black ducks take flight. They take flight going down the river and after that little explosion all I can hear is the mumbling of the current. Something is up ahead of me on the ground. I can't see what but it looks like a dead deer. I get up to it and see that it is a large dog. Oh oh, somebody's dog didn't come home last winter. It's been dead for a long time. As I go by I notice there is a hole in his head and I think that maybe he was put down by his owner or maybe he was caught running deer. In this area if you caught a dog running deer he never came home again. Could be, it was a big dog. I had been walking for about fifteen minutes and I was looking at the other side for a landmark that I knew well, but if I didn't spot it I would go too far.

There is a big walnut I am looking for and that's the only place you can cross the river this time of year. It's like a sand bar. Actually, it's more like a stone bar. You can get across here and only go up to your knees. There it was, the old tree. I rolled up my pants and started. The current pulled at my legs as I made my way to the other side. The bottom was loose stones and you had to be careful or you would find yourself sitting in the river. The river is about thirty-five feet wide at this spot. By the time I got to the other side my legs were about numb. I could hardly feel them. I rolled down my pants and waited for a minute to get some feeling back in my legs. Boy that water was cold.

As I walked along this side I kept a sharp lookout for an old logging trail. It was barely defined along the bank. The timbre had been cut off about sixty years ago from all I had been able to figure out from some of the older men in town. I knew it was right here so kept walking back and forth until I saw a little spot that looked more open. I stepped into the opening and I was right. I could see a path that was almost hidden, but if you look close you could see where it had been a cart path years ago. I walked slow as I knew from other trips that the path had deep ruts that were hidden from view by the ground cover. I don't know what they used to haul out the logs, but it left deep ruts. I followed the trail as best I could for about a mile here again, looking for a sign that I was at the turnoff. There it was, a sharp pointed rock. I turned off to my right and forced my way through the thickets and hard wood stands. As I traveled I listened for the sound of running water. I just sort of felt the right direction as there were no markers of any type. I was always careful not to leave any either. I heard the sound I had been waiting for and, turning more to the right and ahead, I could see the brook. I wanted to come out at one certain spot.

Now I know I am not the only one in the world to love this place. My brother Don knew about it and I am sure many others, but I never met anyone here in over thirty years. Well here I am right at the falls. The trees are almost all spruce and have been growing quietly for maybe a hundred years. They had not been cut, maybe the land owner from years ago saw what I did here? The top of the falls was about ten feet from the surface of the pool below and maybe fourteen feet wide at the top. If you go above the falls you will see that nature has created a funnel affect and a wide spot so that the water will spread out wide enough to cover the whole spread of the falls. I don't think man could have done it for less than a million dollars. I am ashamed to try to measure nature's miracles in this way. When I read this later I may take it out as being a bit overdone. The falls fell over a solid ledge and I could not see any cracks, just moss growing here and there. In the spring, the pool at the bottom of the falls was about five feet deep. Later in the summer the water would hardly be running and only leakage at the end of the pool would keep the brook going at all. Anyone can go to falls that everyone knows about, but it is more meaningful if you have one that's almost hidden. I would like to add and just your own but know that is not true.

By the pool on the other side was a very big stand of swamp Pinks. It was late in the year for them to still be in bloom. I had seen two lady slippers on the way here and by the pool there were large flowered painted trilliums sprinkled here and there. It was getting on to eleven and the sun was starting to get very hot. I baited my hook standing well back and behind a big spruce tree, let out about three feet of line and swung the hook over the pool and let out more line until the hook reached bottom. When fishing small brooks, I use a fly rod so that I can stay back from the fish. In little brooks, trout are real spooky and shadows will make them leave like a shot. I raised the hook off the bottom and move it gently up and down. Wham! Fish on. Now in little brook fishing, which is an acquired taste, you don't wait, you haul your fish out with as little noise as you can. He was a beauty about ten inches and native. Now the water in the Newton Brook is not colorless. It is tinted light brown. I think that it is tannic acid. Don't know, don't care. I have had drinks of water from it my whole life and it tastes fine, I stayed at that pool and took three more trout, the biggest eleven inches. Before I moved on I just sat there and watched the water tumbling over the ledge. The Newton brook trout have the most vivid colors I have ever seen on a native trout anywhere.

I moved on down the brook and caught four more all about nine inches. I was almost at the end where the water gets very deep as it enters the Miller's River. The water gets still and the brook widens out and moves very slowly into the river. I let my bait drift into the still water and just let it lay for a while. Whack! What a hit. I raised the rod and he was big. He came up and rolled and he was the biggest trout I had ever seen in the Newton. There was no room for me to do anything but hang on as he headed for the bank and I tried to turn him but didn't have enough room and he was in the brush and off. I fished there for quite a while after that, but that was all. I sat on the bank for a while and decided I had done enough damage for the day and started home. The sky was starting to look dark and looked like rain and I heard thunder in the distance. I didn't care what it did, I had spent the best part of a day on my favorite brook and marveled again at what nature can do without man. This sort of thing is my Grand Canyon and personal. I felt as though I had made some great decisions about my life that morning but couldn't remember what they were.

In 1939 Mother wanted to see the New York World's Fair. Dad couldn't go. They couldn't afford for both of them to go. They decided that Mom and I should go. Dad said he would take Ken next year. Sis was working as a nurse in a hospital in White Plains, New York and we could stay with her and take the train into the city with only a short walk to the grounds. Up till then I had never even been on a train. Mom asked Miss Elliott, my teacher, if she thought it was alright for me to miss a week of school and she said it would be a very good experience for me.

We both were thrilled by the whole experience. I was lost when we first got there. I had never been in a crowd of more than fifty or so and it made me a little nervous at first. The lines to get into some of the exhibits were very long and a large part of each day were spent in line. The one exhibit I really wanted to see was the Trylon and Perisphere. I had seen them in magazines and they seemed to be the most important. The Trylon had the world's largest escalator and I had never even been on any whatsoever. We went from the Trylon into the Perisphere to see the World of Tomorrow, designed specifically for the people and landscape of the United States. I really loved the General Motors Building. We sat to view the exhibit from moving chairs with individual loudspeakers looking at what was overwhelming for me but exciting. The Ford building was great and touted as what would save the world. I didn't know from what but listened with wonder. The railroad building was great, I could have spent half the time there. They even had R.C.A. with something called television. It was a real picture of what the future would bring. I loved the Chrysler building and the car that talked and even blushed. There was too much to see in the time we were there, but I really enjoyed it. We did not go in the midway part as we had no money for any of the rides or shows. It was a great experience, but I wish I had been a little older. I think I would have got a lot more out of it if I had been of high school age.

We spent the weeknights with Sis, as she worked during the day. She could not get off from work. Every time when we walked from or to the fair we walked through a "colored section" as it was called then. It was the first time I ever saw an alive black man or women. I was a little nervous when we walked at night. Twice we saw tremendous firework shows in the early evening. As far as we knew I probably was the only kid in town to go to the fair. When I got back to school I was asked to speak to all the classes about what I had seen. I could go on forever and I think Miss Elliott got a little sick of the whole thing. She had to shut me off when I went on too long. I'm sure the other pupils were glad when I was through. Be that as it may, it was good for me and that's all I really cared about.

Uncle Luke died in January 1933. He had been quite a man, as we used to say. As a young man, when times got hard on the farm, he got a job on one of the crews building the Hoosick Tunnel, linking Massachusetts to Albany, N.Y. He would come home when he could get off on the weekends and started to see a young lady who lived in Fitzwilliam, N.H. He would travel by horse and buggy up to Fitzwilliam to see her. The story goes that his sister, Delia, didn't like this lady at all. When Luke went up to Fitzwilliam, he went right by the Rev. Tandy's house. Rev. Tandy had a daughter, Ellen, that Luke had known for years. Luke made many trips from home but stopped off at Ellen's house. In retrospect, the folks figured he must have put his horse and buggy in the Rev.'s barn. The Rev. Tandy must have had a real sense of humor because he never said anything to Luke's folks. Well this went on for a while until one day he said he was going to be married in two weeks at the Baptist Church in West Royalston, and of course by the Rev. Tandy. Delia was outraged and I guess so was his other sister, my Grandma Susan. The whole family was upset but of course they all went. Imagine the surprise when Ellen Tandy walked down the aisle. Delia was very upset as she had only a homemade flower arrangement for their wedding gift. Luke put the arrangement on the fireplace hearth in the living room of the farm where everyone would see it, just to remind Delia of her behavior. He kept it there until Delia died in 1929.

Luke and Ellen, we all called her Aunt Nellie, had five children. Florence, John, Bertha, Carl and Lucy. Florence married and moved to California. Bertha married and moved to Fitzwilliam, NH. As a young man, I hardly ever saw them. I saw a lot of Carl. He married and lived in Athol and was the father of three sons: Bill, Ted and Dan, my buddy. Lucy, who Ken and I called Aunt Lucy, I always figured was the old maid type, whatever that is. I had to rethink that impression in time. Now John, Uncle John, was great as far as I was concerned. I used to ride with him on the wagon and he was fun for a kid to be with. I don't know how Ken felt about him as at that age we never held those kinds of discussions, and it's too late to ask him now, but we never seemed to remember folks of that time in our lives in the same light at all. Maybe two years difference in age made a big difference in our perspective. Who knows? When Ken and I use to speak of those folks, it's almost like he knew them from a different slant. Well I can only tell it as I saw it.

John was ten years older than Dad but they were very close. John always thought the world of Dad and they got along very well over the years. They hayed, cut wood, farmed and were very close. I remember John having a team of horses that he was really proud of. He kept the harness polished and in wonderful repair. If you had a team of work horses you were judged by how you took care of them. When we logged off the side hill back of the barn, I remember one young man who worked for us logging with his team. His team was beautiful, not only them, but his harness all shined up with oil and embellished with silver on the bridles. The horses were groomed every night and grained and hayed with care. It was a matter of pride. John's horses were like that. Their barn was much better than ours. It was larger and more modern then ours and the water ran in the water barrel all the time. They also had a tool shed in the barn to repair harnesses and whatever needed work.

I used to love to go over there in the morning and help Aunt Lucy bring in the eggs. She liked me to go with her and answered all my questions. Aunt Nellie was nice but not the brightest coin in the fountain. She died in 1939 at 89. In all fairness, you have to remember that when I knew her she was an old lady and we didn't know how to put a name to the dubious pleasure of growing old. Gee that makes me feel better!? All and all whenever I went over to the Shepardson's I always felt welcome. The Shepardson barn burned down in 1949 and Ken bought the land and I remodeled the new barn for him. He used it as a summer home for a few years, added on and made it his home. He lived in sight of where he was born all his life.

Some of the things that happened when I was young only got straightened out in my mind years later. Aunt Lucy in 1935 was forty-six and we all thought of her as the old maid type. Well up in West Royalston there was a family by the name of Cook. Levi Cook and his wife and five children. The oldest boy, Billy, was blind and lived next door to his father with Vera Fisk. Who at one time taught school. Sis and Don had been taught by her. Of course, that's before she and Billy moved in together. The town would have let her go for that kind of behavior. There was another son, Harry, who I liked very much and became very friendly with him over the years. Next in line was Mary, my age, David, Ken's age and chubby little Alice, the youngest.

Without anyone in the family or the neighborhood knowing, Aunt Lucy and Levi were having an affair. I don't know if anyone knew, all we knew was Dad had heard that Levi Cook had left his wife and five kids. However, John found out that his sister was having an affair. It seems that Lucy used to walk up past the Tandy place and meet Levi in the evening now and then on an old cart path. I'm sure Dad knew and probably told Mom what was going on but we kids didn't know. One day John took his axe and dropped a big tree across the cart path. I don't know how long all this went on. We heard Levi had divorced his wife and Ken and I felt sorry for Mary, David and Alice. We never knew what to say so never mentioned the divorce. I don't seem to remember how long it was when one day Dad came home and said that Aunt Lucy and Levi Cook had just married. It must have been going on for a long time because at that time it took two years before you could remarry if you sued for divorce. It doesn't seem possible that no one knew. I'm glad that Uncle Luke was dead as it would have broken his heart.

Levi moved in and brought the three youngest children to live with them. Uncle John who was fifty-eight at the time was just about out of his mind over the whole thing. Ken and I didn't know what to make of it. The kids seemed all right to us and we treated them like any other new kids. It must have been very hard on them. This whole divorce thing was completely new to us, and I guess we expected the kids to be different somehow, but they were just like any other kids and in no time at all Ken and I were sledding and playing with them. We never had had close neighbors that we played with before.

I think the summer that Aunt Lucy was married was the last summer my friend, Dan, spent at the farm. That was a summer that Dan will remember for the rest of his life. When Dan was there in the summer, he used to help out with the milking and farm chores. One morning he went out to the barn to help Uncle John with the milking. He was surprised to find the big doors closed and opened them to go in. To this day he wishes he had not gone in. There was a big chestnut beam going across the barn from the top of the horse stable to the outside of the barn. There hanging by a logging chain locked around the beam was John. He had climbed up to the beam wrapped the chain around it put the other end around his neck and jumped. I remember it as if it was today. We were just sitting down at the kitchen table when the phone rang. Dad got up and answered it and said, "I'll be right there." He turned from the phone and said to Mother, "I've got to go, John just hung himself." It was the most shocking think I had ever heard in my life and I didn't know how to react. Ken and I went out on the porch and sat there for I don't know how long. For the life of me I don't remember saying a damn thing to him. I don't remember anything of that whole day. I don't remember the funeral as the folks did not take us.

As time went by I overheard Mother and Dad talking and found out that Aunt Nellie thought that she should have known something was wrong as twice when John's laundry was done there had been a mark on his long underwear as if he had been standing in the water for a long time up to his chest. Mother figured that he was trying to get up his courage to drown himself. It makes sense to me but we will never know. As the years went by, I heard a lot more from Don and Sis. They were not there but knew Uncle John differently then I as they were much older. Aunt Lucy had been raped as a young girl, fifteen or sixteen. She was a friend of Vera Fisk who taught school at the bottom of Beamis' Hill. The school was on Stewart Road. There was a short cut through the woods back of the Shepardson's farm and Lucy had gone down it to see Vera after school was out. Well she came home with her clothes torn all to pieces and told her folks that a man had raped her. Of course, there was a hunt for him immediately. No one was ever found. Over the years it seemed to some people in the family that the relationship between John and Lucy was almost too close for brother and sister. It seems that this was never really discussed, just noticed. John was very protective of her and she never had any men friends. Sis and Don always thought that Dad knew something was not just right, but no one really knew. It would explain a lot but it will ever remain as it should, in doubt. After this tragic episode, I didn't go over just to visit. For some reason having Levi and the kids there made it impossible for me to be comfortable with Aunt Lucy. She remained married to him for the rest of her life. The middle son, David, was epileptic and sometime in the nineteen fifties he had a spell when they were cutting their fire wood to length and he fell into the saw and was killed. It was the same saw rig that we had used for years to cut our wood. The two girls married and moved on with their lives. In all the years since, I never discussed John's suicide with Dan. I wanted to but something always held me back. At the time, I was only nine years old and no one wanted to talk about it with me. Why he killed himself bothered me for years. Many years later I found out from Mom that John had told Dad he was having sex with his sister Lucy.

June 3, 1940 was not a good day for me. Nothing went right. When I took the cow up to the well for water she stepped on my foot. Unless that has happened to you, you have no idea how much it hurts. Her foot is split and it slides off dragging the pain out. A hell of a way to start the day. It was Tuesday and we had a math test and I wasn't prepared at all. That really wasn't the day's fault, just mine. I got into a fight with my best friend Bob Smith over a jackknife that was mine and he broke, and Miss Elliot sent me out of the room for a while to think about my behavior. I thought about it but came to no helpful conclusion. The math test was awful and I am sure I failed it. When Ken and I got home I got into it with Mother about getting some manure for her flower garden. I hated to take the wheelbarrow down under the barn and load it up and then spread it for Mother in her garden.

Dad was home and the Reverend Nylan and his wife stopped by to say hello to Mother and Dad.

They played bridge together quite often. Mother was in the garden talking with them and I went back to the house to feel sorry for myself. When I walked into the house I met Dad in the kitchen and he asked who had just come into the yard. I told him and he told me to tell them that he had an awful headache and would they please excuse him as he was not very good company at the moment. He said he was going to lie down for a while and went into the bedroom. Dad skipped supper that night and we all went to bed early. I had trouble going to sleep that night. I just couldn't shut my mind off.

That night, June 4, 1940, about one in the morning, my Mother shook me awake in tears." Wake up, Tuddy, I think your Father is dead. I was in a complete daze as I went downstairs and into the bedroom where they slept. Dad was laying on his back and looked fine, and I didn't know what to do. I tried to wake him by calling his name and felt almost uncontrollable panic. The next thing I remember was sitting in the kitchen with Mother. Mother, who had always been the strong one in an emergency, was falling completely apart and I didn't know what to do. After a while I saw Ken sitting in one of the kitchen chairs, I don't know when he came in, if Mother went to get him or what, he was just there.

Mother went to the phone and called a doctor, I don't know who. I just remember someone that I didn't know coming in and telling us that he was gone.

It was starting to become light, and Mother looked awful and really could not stop sobbing. Then all of a sudden, she sat up and said that she must call Sis and Don and all the family. I was starting to feel that my life was over. Life as I knew it, as it turned out, was. Mother called everyone and around ten a hearse came from Athol and they put my father on a stretcher and carried him away. About eleven Bill Gillis arrived. He was crying so hard that I hardly knew him. He held Mother and they both cried. I could not cry, I think, because I really didn't believe it yet. I don't think Ken cried either. Bill stayed for two hours or more, Mother was afraid to let him go in the condition he was in. Several more of Dad's friends came. I can't remember who, I was still in a daze. We got through the day somehow and Aunty came that night. She was an absolute wreck. She was close to having hysterics, not close, she did, and I tried to comfort her. I finally got her calmed down when Aunt Sadie arrived, and that was worse. Dad's two sisters depended on Dad for the world as they knew it. I always felt that Ken and I sort of fell by the wayside for a time.

Dad's body was brought back to the house and set out in the bay window in Grandma's living room for the funeral. Don and Sis arrived along with everyone Dad had known. It seemed to me hundreds came and I had a very hard time at the funeral. It was really dawning on me that he was gone. I stood by Dad to say good bye with my cousin Russell. He put his arm around me and said, "Do you think you will ever be half the man that he was?" I have tried to be that much of a man but feel I never made it. Even now I am almost crying as I write this. My sister NeNe was wonderful and great with Mother. Don was very quiet. The next day Mom, Sis, Don and Bill with Ken and I were sitting on the back porch when down at the end of the flat three deer came out and just stood there looking at the house. Well that did it for Bill, who had had a few drinks, and he said, "My God they were saying good bye to Eri." He jumped in his car and off he went. Everyone tried to stop him but you don't stop a six-foot three Irishman when he wants to go. Sis and I chased after him in Aunty's car for a while but lost him on a dirt road. We were afraid he would drive off the road and hurt himself. The next few days were a blur. I went back to school in four days.

I was graduating in three weeks from the eighth grade. Five girls and three boys. Those three weeks seem to be gone from my memory. We had a ceremony at town hall and a little speech we each had to give on our future. It was sheer agony for me and I got through it but with very little expression I am sure. There just didn't seem to me to be any future. There was no insurance, no Social Security, there just was no money, except what was owed to Dad from all over by people he had advanced credit to for everyday needs from his Raleigh business. We did have a closet full of the products he sold, but that wasn't worth very much. I had no idea what we were going to do but I wanted to stay right here. I would work for someone and make enough money for us to live on. Whatever was going to happen, I wasn't asked. I was fifteen, who cared? I just knew that Mother and Aunty were talking about what to do and it was driving me crazy. I think Ken and I sort of fell apart from each other for a while, each with his own agony inside. Aunty was with us that summer and was a wreck. Sis and Don had to go back to work. We gave Dad's canoe to Bill and he used it till it just fell apart. I got so I wanted to be alone and took Dads 250/3000 rifle and disappeared in the wood for hours. Mother thought that I was headed for trouble and got Don to take the rifle away with him. I had

had visions of living in the woods and to hell with them all. I still had not cried. I don't remember Ken and I talking about Dad's death until years later. I suppose it probably seems funny to anyone else, but we each had our own fears and apprehensions. We just couldn't talk about it.

About three weeks into the summer we got a call from W. W. Williams who lived down the road from the Whittfield place. Buck and Mrs. Whittfield had died a few years ago and Herbert Graves had had life tenancy in the house. Herbert had fallen downstairs and Williams had found him at the bottom dead. Dad was gone so Mother was to be the executor of the estate. It seems that W. W. Williams who lived up the road had stopped that morning to get his milk and found him dead at the bottom of the stairs. The State Police arrived and decided it was an accident and there was no investigation other than this brief visit. My brother Don thought differently. He was at the farm and went up that morning when the police were there and told them there were a lot of Herb's guns missing and that there was a pool of blood around Herb's head and it didn't seem right as there didn't seem to be any on the stair where his head struck. It looked to him as if he had been struck on the head from behind. Well the Police who more or less said that they were the experts wanted no part of that and declared the investigation over, called the medical examiner, took his report and that was the end of poor Herb.

Mother was meticulous in settling the estate. Mother, Ken and I did it all. Mother brought a big notebook and she followed the lawyer's advice and cataloged everything in the house, now I mean everything. We started in the attic and moved down through the bedrooms, living room, kitchen and so on. It took us about a week. The first thing we found of interest to Ken and I was a wooden box full of dynamite caps. We knew what they were but not how to safely dispose of them. W. W. Williams stopped by and Mother told him about them. He said he would show us how to take care of them the right way. He knew damn well what we wanted to do with them. There was about ten of them all tied together in the box. He took us out in the front yard and put the box on a stone wall across the road. He got his 22 rifle out of the car and told us to stay back and shot the box. I think he misjudged a little. There was one hell of a bang and little pieces of stone rained down on us for a bit. It sure made Mother jump. We thought it was great fun. She was a bit upset but mothers are like that. We found a double barrel muzzle loading shot gun and a bag of number nine shot and half a keg of black powder. We never told Mother about the powder and had a great time with the old muzzle loader. There was also an electric therapy machine with wands in several sizes and a book on how to use it. We could never make it work.

As I think about it now, maybe Don was right about Herb being murdered. We never did find any of his guns. W. W. Williams was a very interesting man and later in life I use to stop at his house to talk and see how he was doing. He had put up a sign on the corner of Jacob's Hill and the Falls Road advertising himself as the Country Cooper. Well I had to see what that was all about, and I was pleasantly surprised to see that he had a lot of talent along those lines. He did all kinds of copper work and wood baskets. They were works of art. Over the years we became very friendly and he told me he had invented a tool for wood working and he was applying for a patent and would show me what it was maybe next time he saw me.

It was about two years later when my brother Don and I were hunting birds up that way and we stopped in to see him. He said that he was in production and they were being manufactured for him in a New York factory. What he had invented was a bit for a router that had a slot in it so that you could put all different shapes of cutters in. It came in a neat kit with ten different sizes and shapes. It looked to me as a very clever idea. He said that it was just starting to sell and he would like me to have a set and let him know what I thought of it as it was right down my alley. Well it was, as I was a building contractor and used routers quite often. The first time I used it was on a house I built on Chestnut Hill in Athol. It had a blade with it to cut Formica and I tried it cutting a counter edge prior to finishing it by hand. Look out Nellie! The damn slotted router shaft split and the blade took off and went right through the kitchen wall on the other side of the room. Well it had been a gift but could have been deadly, so I thought I should tell him what happened because that was one dangerous tool and should be corrected or taken off the market.

I went to see him that night and he was not happy and told me I must have done something wrong and that it could not happen as I had told him. I had brought him both pieces and you could see that the material was at fault. He gave me a new bit and said try this one. I didn't argue with him but, believe me, I never tried it again. I had visions of it going into my stomach instead of the wall. I was looking at my old tool chest just the other day and found it and threw it out. I had forgotten all about it. Well he was clever, but that item was taken off the market before it killed someone.

Well back to the Whittfield estate. Buck had the best toolshed I ever saw for the times. Even today it would be tremendous for a farm workshop. Old Buck Whittfield had been a carpenter and a damn good one his entire life. His shop was completely equipped. There were no power tools but if they were sold today the tool collectors would have been in heaven and the bidding high. There were no living relatives and after all debts and the lawyers were paid, whatever was left was Mother's. There had to be an auction held and we hired Uncle Watson's brother who had a reputation as a very fine auctioneer. Of course, "HE DRANK" just like Uncle Watson. Mother was a little worried about this and I told her I would keep an eye on him the day of the auction.

During the auction Mother kept track of everything and only sent out enough to cover the debts and what she didn't want. The auctioneer would stop now and then and go into the toolshed and take out a little bottle and refresh himself. I watched him like a hawk, but he seemed to just get faster and better. He was really good and could get the last cent out of a New England farmer. Two days did it and we had a lot of stuff left over. Anything that would be sold now, Mother would get the money, and believe me, she would get the best price going. Mother found very little money, as I remember only about four hundred in bills. All the beds had been sold and most of the furniture. In Mrs. Whittfield's bedroom there had been some wicker furniture and Mother had kept it as someone wanted to buy it. Mother couldn't figure out where Mrs. Whittfield's gold watch was, and she knew there should be some other money. Of course, Herb had been there for several years and maybe he had spent it. I went into the bedroom with Mother and noticed a little table that use to stand by her bed.

All of a sudden, I remembered Mrs. Whittfield opening a little drawer built into the corner and getting me a fifty-cent piece for the suckers I use to bring her. I opened it and it was full of fifty cent pieces. As I mentioned, I kept that table. Mother told me it was my table from now on. There was a little drawer in all four corners and in one was money and her gold watch. Again, it was all fifty cent pieces, with some very old ones mixed in. Today they would have been worth a lot more than fifty cents. In the last draw, there was eight fifty-dollar gold coins. I guess the total money found might have been six hundred. Mother gave me the gold watch and I sold it to buy a chromatic Harmonica the next year. One of the most interesting things we had left was an Edison phonograph with a big horn that played wax cylinders. There were a lot of cylinders and it played great. We played it for years and Ken had it with him until it wore out years later.

Somewhere up in my attic I use to have a copy of all the things that were in the house and what they sold for. When I sold my house, I wish I'd saved it as it would be fun to see how prices have changed. I think after the Whittfield house was sold in 1940 and all the bills were paid that Mother got around four thousand dollars out of the whole deal. It doesn't sound like very much when you think of it as the life of the Whittfields, but for those days it was quite a lot. I liked Mrs. Whittfield and she added a little color in my life as did her father Buck. When Mother died in 1974, as I remember, she left around eight thousand dollars.

The old Whittfield place still stands today and I go by it to go hunting once and a while. I miss the little house that Buck built to stand in out of the weather at the bottom of the hill while waiting for the mail. The house has been poorly maintained and unless someone gives it some care soon it won't be worth the effort. The old Falls Road it stands on is in terrible repair and only four houses on it to the New Hampshire line are left. Come to think of it, that's about all there ever was. It's really too bad that the road has been let go as it is the road to Royalston Falls. I was there about four years ago with my oldest son Gary and his son, my grandson, Jeremy. There is a path off the road to go see the falls, but you will need four-wheel drive to go over the road to get to the path. The town has seventy miles of road and a big percentage of that is dirt. The town has a hard time taking care of the roads where there are kids that go to school. The population is only about thirteen hundred and it was about the same in 1940. Even so, if you have four-wheel drive or a lot of courage, you should see the falls. It is a wild place and the stairs that use to go down around it have been gone for years. There is another way to go in, but it is not half as interesting. You can always go see Doane's Falls, easy to get to but not as wild and untouched. There is another fall called Cascade Falls, also called Spirit Falls. You walk in quite a way for that one, but only go when there has been a wet spell as it doesn't look like much in dry weather.

After Dad died, that first summer was hard on Ken and me. No one told us anything and we worried about what would happen to us. Mother did say she was not selling the farm, so that gave us some feeling of security. Dad had always raised gladiolas and they were growing very tall. There was a very large collection of bulbs, maybe ten or so colors, and they were growing beautifully this summer. Dad always cut large bouquets and gave them to friends and folks that he sold produce to. Before they left for their homes, he would bring a large bouquet for them to take home. A gesture like that was so typical of him. He loved the flowers and wanted to share their beauty with all. That was my Dad. When we sold the farm in the late fifties, I took all the bulbs with me and raised them for about twenty years. I became a contractor and did custom homes and additions. I loved the glads and was very careful to take good care of them each winter. They had to be dug up and dried each fall and treated for dry rot and stored where it was dry for the winter. I raised them for about twenty years but I lost them all one winter. In the spring when I got them out to plant they had all turned soft and all were dead. I never raised them again. It took all the joy out of it as new bulbs would not mean the same to me. Like my Dad I took bouquets of glads to my customers who I considered friends. It was what my Dad had done so it was what I did. Simple, isn't it? Or maybe it's just in the genes and I couldn't help it.

The summer went on fast, and one day Aunty and Mother called Ken and I into the kitchen and told us what was planned. We were going to move to Gardner and go to school there. Aunty had found a place to live and we would all live together. I became a problem for everybody, I hated the idea of leaving the farm. It was my home and I'd be damned if I would leave. My older brother Don and I had a big scrap over it and almost came to blows over the whole thing. Of course, I had to surrender, but not before I made everyone's life miserable including mine.

Mother promised that we would spend every summer at the farm and some weekends. We had to close up the farm and that meant we had do something about our six rabbits. There were three angoras and three plain white short hair. We talked it over with our brother Don and he thought the best thing was to shoot them. Ken didn't want to kill them so we decided to just let them go. Don said they would probably die in the woods. It probably wasn't the thing to do but at the moment it seemed best. About three years later I met a man hunting on our land and he said that there were some funny looking rabbits in the woods around the farm. I didn't say a word but knew why and felt better about leaving them. I had been afraid they all would have died in the wild. Looked like they did well.

Two days before we left the farm I woke up hurting all over and found myself at the bottom of the stairs. I evidently jumped to my feet and ran out into the night. Mom and Aunty had been in the living room and had heard me so came after me. I felt like I was in a different world and couldn't get back, and what was I doing out in the middle of the lawn and at night? I couldn't figure how I had got there. I had no memory of anything, just finding myself in the field and Mother and Aunty telling me that I must have been walking in my sleep and had fallen down the stairs. I had a lump on my head and various bruises, but other than that I was fine. I was just terribly confused. They had me sit up awhile but I felt very tired and finally they told me to go to bed. I went upstairs to bed and later woke up crying. Everything all of a sudden seemed too much. In the morning, I felt better than I had all summer. For several months after this sleep walking I would have a hard time falling asleep. I was afraid I would do it again but I never did. Mother rented Grandma's side of the house to a local family for the next year and that was it. End of summer, end of my life too, I thought, so we moved.

The house that Aunty and Mother decided on was in walking distance of the high school and the elementary, so it was good for both Ken and I to get to school. It was the second story of a house on Elm Street which consisted of five rooms. Three bedrooms, living room and kitchen. For whatever reason, Mother wanted Ken and I to each have our own room. There was a big walk-in closet that had an outside window and Mother thought Ken could make a bedroom out of it. I must be honest. I didn't think about that at all. It was years later that I found out that Ken had hated it and blamed me for the whole thing. When he told me how he had felt I felt terrible but it was twenty years after the fact and a little late for regrets. Things of a like nature that happened as time went on bothered Ken and he never forgot or forgave. I wish I had been able to see what was going on in his life, but it went right by me. I felt lost but all kids do when going into a new school and new environment. The enrollment was nine hundred in 1940 and seemed scary to me. Aunty had picked my courses and I was all set to start. Well I did and was totally lost for a while. I had one advantage. I knew some of the women teachers as Aunty had brought some of them to the farm to visit. I don't know if having Aunty teaching there helped me or not.

As time went on I found that I rather liked this new school. Everything seemed pretty easy except something called algebra. It seemed that the other kids had had a start in elementary school but I had no idea what the hell it was all about. That was my cross to bear, I hated it from day one and that never changed. I drove my teacher crazy. I realize now that most of my problems were my own fault. No one can teach a closed mind. Aunty helped me all the time with my homework in math and I got through without failing it. I told Aunty I wasn't going to take math next year. Ken seemed to do pretty well and the year passed quickly. Whenever we could we went to the farm on weekends in good weather. I took time off from school to hunt deer and Mother signed for me. The principal told me that it wasn't an acceptable excuse. I didn't mention it to Mom and I guess he didn't either as I did it every year. Ken and I got through the year and could hardly wait to get home to the farm.

That's when we decided to do our own mowing and sell the hay. We had our problems with the mowing and it's a wonder we didn't get seriously hurt or kill each other. We put in a small garden and raised our gladiolas. They had to be in the ground every year. The haying really wasn't worth what we put ourselves through, and we only did it the first two years. After that we had someone cut it for the hay. That first summer was hard. We really needed money and I decided to see if I could hire out during haying season. I called Hollis Chace and he said he could use me for about four weeks. He was going to be haying up our way at several farms and would pick me up each morning at five thirty. When he was working at the other end of the town, Aunty said she would take me and pick me up. That was the hardest four weeks in my life to date. When Hollis worked everyone worked. He was a hard man but I liked him. I had known him all my life and gone to school with three of his kids. I was told that summer was one of the hottest we had had in years. When we brought the hay to the barns it had to be forked into the mows. I would be told to get up in the mow to take away as it was forked up to me. It got so hot that you felt like you were in your own world. There were two other men working for Hollis and they were very strong and full of hell.

I remember when we were haying out behind Millie French's house just off the common near where her laundry had been hung out to dry. We were all turning hay to dry in the hot sun and you could see a line of drying clothes back of the house. I was working beside Henry Clemens who was pushing hard to finish. After a while he stopped and leaned on his pitchfork and said with a big grin, "My God look at that, there are Millie's pants hanging on the line." That was in reference to white bloomers that looked long enough to come to your knees. I'm glad Millie didn't hear him. Henry Clemens was the strongest and he would try to outdo Hollis. He couldn't and Hollis was twenty years older than Henry. Hollis worked his men and his horses hard. It was good for me to be with these men. They had all known Dad and treated me as one of them. That was very important to me at that time in my life. When I was working away I guess Ken did whatever Mother wanted. To tell the truth I was too tired to pay much attention to what he did. We had a lot of strawberries to pick that summer and Mother decided that she would sell them door to door in Athol. Ken and I hated that with a passion, but we needed the money and got more selling this way then when we sold to the stores. She also tried to collect from the folks that still owed on their Raleigh bill. I don't think she ever got it all but I'll bet if she was alive today she could tell you who still owed her. Mother never forgot things like that. She always paid her bills and expected everyone else to do the same. I was glad when we sold the last of the berries.

We did get in some great fishing and sometimes not doing very much at all. We saw a lot of Madam as she came down the road to see Mother all the time. As I look back on that summer it feels as if I had not really been there except maybe as sort of an observer. I don't know if you will understand what I mean or not. I can't seem to remember many of the details as they went by so fast. The summer was over in a wink and we had to go back to school.

Sis had been at the farm on vacation and had been dating a man, George Glasson, from Orange. I don't think Ken liked him very much. Then we no sooner got back to Gardner then Sis told us she was going to be married. They decided to spend their first winter at the farm. I had my driver's license and thought I could tease Aunty to let me use her car to go up to the farm and see them. She let me go a few times and I got in some bird hunting. George and I got along pretty well. George had a job at Athol Manufacturing where they made artificial leather. He had never done any hunting to speak of and I thought I would sort of introduce him to gun safety and handling. Well he bought an 870 Remington Wingmaster and I took him hunting with me a few times. He was all thumbs with a gun in his hands. He was very careless and dangerous and had several accidental discharges that scared the hell out of me. I tried but I never could get him to keep his fingers off the trigger. I finally gave up and decided not to hunt with him because he was too dangerous. He went with Don and I one time and a bird got up on Don's far right and he killed it. All of a sudden George stuck his head up out of the brush and said that was kind of close to him. He was supposed to be on the other side of us and how he got there we will never know. He could get lost in his own back yard and had no sense of direction in the woods. He took off his hat and there was a little trickle of blood coming down his forehead. He had been hit by a pellet. Don and I didn't tell Sis for years and when we did she was mad at us for several more years. Guns were not for him.

Years later I went up to see them when they lived on Betty Spring Road in Gardner and I happened to look into their fireplace and saw a big dent in the metal heatilator in the back of the fireplace. I said, "George, what the hell is that?" He looked kind of sheepish and said, one night Sis was taking a bath and he decided to clean his gun. Somehow, he figured he would put a shell through it. Why I don't know but he put in a slug. The bath was almost behind the fireplace and somehow it went off. He said Sis came wet and naked out of that bathroom like she was being chased by the hammers of hell. George grinned and said, "My God I couldn't hear for damn near an hour." That probably was lucky as Sis must have been pretty loud for a while. Well that did it for me. I never took him hunting again.

About three weeks after they had been married and living up at the farm, I got a call from Percy Chase and he told me that their friends were going to give them a housewarming party and that it would be next weekend on Saturday night. Of course, we all went and it was a lot of fun. Percy got me to one side and told me to go down to the barn and get a handful of hay. Well I knew better but did it anyway. He sneaked into their bedroom and put it down under the blankets at the foot of the bed. The party broke up around one in the morning and we all went home. It was not a pleasant bed time. From what George said, Sis was very tired and when she stretched out and hit the hay in the bed there was an explosion. Not a good night. It must have been ten years before I told her that I had anything to do with it. One night after a few drinks I told her and I think she was still mad at me years later. She knew it had been Percy right off and up until then I had left it alone. I was perfectly willing for Percy to take the blame. I'll never know why I told her. I guess my conscience must have bothered me. She said she had never believed that I had anything to do with it. She sure made me feel bad.

I never got very good marks as I found I could just sail along without doing homework and still pass. Here again I found that being able to read and retain what I read was the way to go. I had one period of woodworking and found my life's work. I loved it and would have stayed in that class all day if I could. The instructor was Dean Johnson who I admired and who became my friend for life. When I had a study period I got permission to spend it back in woodworking class. I did this for four years and knew what I wanted for my life's work. Not teaching but building. Dean built his own house near the school and I use to help him when he would allow it. His wife was called Fanny and she was lovely. I did not know at the time that she was dying of cancer. Life will never be predictable as some folks seem to think. About eight years later, Dean use to date my Mother. Aunty had known him for years and I think it bothered her a bit to see him going out with Mother. He was very handsome and a really charming man. He had a phrase that I will always remember as he was the only man I ever heard use it. When teaching he loved to use the term HOW SOME EVER. I loved it and always think of him using that whenever he could fit it in. When he used it, it was like one word.

All at once my whole outlook changed. On December 7, 1941 the Japanese attacked Pearl Harbor. I remember the next day at school as we listened to the President talking on the loudspeaker system. It took several days for most of us students to realize what it meant for us. Four seniors left right off and went into the military. Before the end of the year five or six more left. Everyone started to think of their life in a different manner. A lot of us thought the war would be over before we graduated. Mother would never sign for me to go early and made that very clear right from the start. The year dragged on with all of us listening to the President's fireside chats, all of us on edge. I felt lost as I'm sure most of us did. For me I just promptly lost interest in school. I never did any homework again. How the hell I passed I'll never know, but I did. I got nervous, I got hives, I got a girlfriend.

I went out for football. I had seen two games played the year before and they were the first I had ever seen. Talk about being green, I had absolutely no idea what it was all about and tried to hide that fact. They let me play in practice and I was put in the back field, whatever that meant. If anyone got through the line with the ball I stopped them. I was pretty good at that. Then one day the coach got upset about the first team over the way they were hitting and decided to work them. He had all of us learners stand in a line and had the first team run at us and take us out. I don't know what that did for their ability as he had two men hit us, one high and one low. We were just supposed to stand there and get hit. Any damn fool could hit you if you just stood there and it would hurt your back when you were hit. I was beginning to realize that I was not much of a team player. When that was over I showered and told the coach that it was not my idea of learning a damn thing about the game and I had better things to do.

He said that I should stay as he had seen me on the field and thought I would be pretty good as time went on. As far as I was concerned time had just gone on and I left the team. It was just as well as I would have had to give up hunting in the fall. My marks, believe it or not, were acceptable. At least not failing, and I was thinking of trying to find a job for after school. Dean Johnson got me some work painting inside of two old homes that were for sale and I did a real good job and started to get quite a lot of work along that line.

Now Dean was a very handsome man and he had lost his wife the year before and I guess he was considered fair game. There was a teacher, Miss Whittier, who was not pretty but kept all the young boys looking and I think a lot of older ones too. She had a hell of a figure, a bust line like, well what the kids today call awesome. Now you have to remember this was the forties when boobs were molded to startling points. She also had a great butt. It seemed that whenever she had a study class she had a problem with her door sticking or her window would be stuck. Instead of calling the janitor she would call Dean and ask him to help her. A lot of us had seen this happen and we all knew she was after him one way or another. She was a real sexy woman and we all knew it and wondered. It just happened that her study class was the same period that I had wood class. It was obvious that Dean wanted no part of her. He solved it by sending me up to her classroom to help her. She liked all males but would be disappointed and then be right behind me while I opened the window or fixed whatever terrible problem she had. After I went to help her a couple of times she stopped calling him. After that she would try to waylay him in the halls. He always came in early but she started to show up at his class room and he started to come in as late as he could.

After a while I sort of forgot the whole thing, till one day I had to work on the stage to build some flats for a play the senior class was putting on. It was one of the jobs that the wood classes did for the school and I liked it. I went up to the stage and came in the back way and was just going out to get the plans when I heard someone sort of groaning and I stopped and looked behind what flats had been set up. Oh my! There was Miss Whittier with her back toward me and her skirt around her waist and her steins around her ankles and Mr. Coogan, our music teacher, was holding on with both hands. All I could think of was the old poem, "His pants were down, her ass was bare, if he wasn't fucking her then why was he there?" I guess I have a mean streak in me. They were too involved to see me so I backed away and left the stage. But I just couldn't help it, I slammed the door. I wished I could have seen what happened. God, it must have been a picture worth a thousand words. I wanted to tell Dean but I only did years after and I thought he would choke on his laughter. I never told anyone else and it was very hard not to. I should have gone to someone in charge as Coogan, who was married, ran off with a high school senior that he got pregnant my senior year. At the time I felt that if I had told Dean, maybe he would have told the powers that be, but I doubt it. Years later when I told Aunty she wasn't as surprised as I thought she would be and said that Coogan had been in trouble before with women.

Sis and George had moved to Gardner and George was working in a hardware store. Sis had gone back to work as a nurse at the Gardner State Hospital where they had a cottage as part of her salary. George never knew when he would be drafted, so their future was always a little cloudy. He was called up in 1942 and spent twenty-three months overseas. Mother wanted me to join a group from Gardner to entertain the troops, so I did, and about twenty-five of us went to Fort Devens once a month to put on our individual acts. I wore kilts and sang the Harry Lauder songs, I think fairly well, I hope. Most of the kids that went were friends. Angelo Solienus was a very good friend, and in the back of the bus coming home at night, oh my. He and I had a lot of fun with a couple of gals. Mother was in the front of the bus and l let her get off by herself in front of our house, and I stayed on with Angelo. We would get off later and walk the gals home and then walk the railroad tracks back. Of course, after a few long goodnight kisses. Mother was not very happy over the whole thing, but I lived with it.

The year went very fast and Mother and I both got a job working in Union Twist Drill in Athol for the summer. I ran whatever I was told to between departments. It was like watching the leaves turn without a frost. I thought I would go crazy before the summer was over. I knew one thing and that was I would never work in a place like that. I needed more than that kind of boredom. I don't know how those men could stand it. They would make one operation on a drill or mandrel or whatever and pass it on to the next operation. What a thrill, no wonder so many of them drank. I never felt I earned my pay when I was there. I was glad when the summer was over and actually looked forward to school. I can hardly believe I wrote that, but it's true. Imagine me being glad to go back to school.

The school year started fine and a damn pretty girl asked me to a dance. I said yes but I had no more idea how to dance then a cow knew how to skate. I had been taking music from Mr. Cogan and the dance was his idea for his music students. I had been asked to sing in kilts at the school assembly twice and maybe that's where she saw me. I didn't know her at all. Well that's how that started, we were inseparable for the next two years. We were always together whenever we could be. She was a year younger than me so maybe that's why I had never met her. Her name was Marjorie French and I was at her house most of my spare time. Her father was a Major in the Army Postal Service and had been Superintendent of Mails in Gardner before joining the Army. Her brother was in the Navy as a medic. Her mother and older sister worked at Heywood's, who manufactured materials for the war. It was rather odd as Margie's sister Barbara was also dating a man by the name of Stewart. We were not related in any way. They got married and he went into the Marines. He was a good guy but drank way too much. Margie's brother

Fred was married to a very little gal called Stubby, and I liked her a lot. We became great friends. However, she had a big problem with her new mother-in-law. When Margie's Mom, Ethel, found out that her son Fred was engaged she took to her bed for a week. Poor Stubby, she had to face that kind of attitude the rest of her married life and I can tell you, it was hell on her. They got married and Fred went overseas. Margie and Stubby both used to come up to the farm on weekends and stay at the farm with us all.

That winter in the middle of a very bad storm back in Gardner, Ken and I were looking out the window and we saw Mr. Kelly, who lived just up the street, get blown right off his feet and into a big drift of snow. He totally disappeared and we stood there watching and he did not get up. He was a very frail old man and what he was doing out in that storm I'll never know. Ken and I grabbed our coats and went out to get him. He could not get up and looked very sick and cold. We got him up and took him up the street to his house and rang the bell. He had a housekeeper and I don't think she even knew he was out. She was very upset and we helped her get him upstairs and she said she would take care of him and we went home.

Several days later after the storm, we got a telephone call from the housekeeper that Mr. Kelly wanted to see us. Ken and I went over to see him and he told us that he thought we had saved his life. He said he had given up just before we arrived and knew he could not get up. We stayed a while and talked about all kinds of things. I really don't remember the conversation as he pretty well controlled it. He was a very positive old man and mostly we just listened. Somewhere along the way he found out I was looking for a part time job after school. He tried to give us some money but both Ken and I refused. Hell, we would have done the same for the neighbor's dog. I forgot all about it when a few days later I got a call from his housekeeper. She told me that if I still wanted a job I should go over to Kelly Brother's Chair Factory and see Mr. Kelly's son Francis, who was the owner. I did and he gave me an after-school job stuffing cushions. This was the first time I had ever seen how cushions were made. You put them together in a machine, springs and padding, then close them in and fit the cover over the opening and the machine pushes the whole works into the cover. After this they go to be stitched up and they were done. I was paid two dollars an hour. There were two men doing the same thing and I got into trouble. I had no idea how they were paid and tried to do as many as I could each day.

The second week I was there the foreman called me to one side. He tried to explain that the other men were working piece work and I was going to upset the whole thing and that the whole job would be revaluated and a new rate set. I was starting to learn things about the work place that I would rather not know. I would have thought that if you were on piece work that the harder you worked and the more you produced the more you would be paid. It doesn't work that way. The other men were doing all they wanted to and didn't want me to screw up the rate by producing too many. I was learning how the world worked and I didn't like it at all. It wasn't a great introduction into the chair industry, at least not for me. I damn sure wasn't going to do this much longer as summer was coming and I would have to decide what I was going to do for work this summer as I had been drafted and would be going into the service in September. My brother Don said he could get me a job at S.W. Cards in Mansfield, Massachusetts. He was the foreman of the lathe department and the shop was very busy. They made taps and dies and had a big order going to Russia. He lived in Mansfield, about three hours from Gardner, and said

I could live with him and his wife Evelyn. They had a little girl Marcia, my niece, who was four and they were expecting another child soon. He said he could get me a job in packing and shipping. Don and I got along very well. He and his friend Bob Bridges had a hunting camp on the Bear's Den Road in Athol and I went hunting with them every year in the fall.

It was decided that it would be the best chance I would have for a summer job, so I went to Mansfield. It was war time and you had to be finger printed and have a badge with your picture on it and always have it on your shirt. The plant was guarded and you were checked in and out each day. I found the plant well run and the war effort was really pushing the men to produce. It was a lot different than working in a chair plant. We packed thousands of taps in little wooden boxes three to a box. It took three different taps to thread a hole, a plug, a taper, and a bottermer. They would come down from the finishing room in big boxes, all each type in its own box and you put three, one of each type, in a wooden box. Sounds easy but when you got to the end and it didn't come out right, you would have to open every box until you found your mistake.

I did fine, but one day they moved me up on the third floor and told me to pack three thousand taps. I spent two days packing but it didn't come out right. The last three taps were one plug and two tapers. Oh my God, what to do. There were all those little boxes piled up in stacks and I wanted to find the mistakes before I got caught. It didn't happen. I got caught when they checked on me at the end of the third day. The foreman was not happy, but I think I felt worse. He was very calm and just told me to find the mix up and fix it. I worked one whole day and never found one wrong one. I was beginning to think that they had been wrong from the start. Then I found one wrong. It took almost the second day to find the other.

I got through that problem and went right on into another. In the room downstairs where I was packing most of the time, there was a line of women that inspected taps and dies before they were sent up to be polished. Sometimes we would get an order for a shipment and I would take a wheeled truck and bring them down. Now in that line of women there was one really cute gal and she flirted with all, but I thought more with me. When you came down from upstairs you had to go right by the gals and she always looked so damn neat and smiled and all that jazz. Right in the middle of the wide hall was a big structural post that helped hold up the second floor. Well you know what I did, I grinned back at her and went right into the post and about a thousand small taps went flying on the floor. The foreman was not so nice about this. In fact, he was furious, to say the least. I never felt so stupid in my life. The damned post I ran into was painted red and was about a foot thick. You almost had to have your head up your ass to hit it. All the taps had to go back upstairs to be inspected as they could be chipped. I got through the day and hoped Don didn't find out, but of course he did and it was a long time before anyone would let me forget it. As you can see, I never did. What the hell did I learn out of that, keep your eye on the prize but make sure you know what the prize is, or should be?

Don and I went trout fishing several times and I enjoyed being with him. Evelyn and I got along fine and, all in all, it was a pretty good summer and I made some money to help out. Don and Bob Bridges, who also worked there, took me to see what was called a naughty movie at an outdoor theater. I had never seen an outdoor theater and I thought it was a good way to go to the movies. As far as the movie we saw it was by today's standards pretty mild. It was called The Sins of Bali and the native women were naked to the waist. The story line was terrible but a titty show in the forties was unheard of. My first so called adult film. Don also took me to see wrestling for the first time. I thought it was real and couldn't believe it when Don told me it was all a fake. All and all it was a very good summer for me and I think I matured somewhat?

I left for the farm two weeks before my senior year started. I didn't tell Mother or Aunty I was coming home. I took the train but I forgot how I was to get home from Athol. When I got there, I saw Frappy French and his old Ford truck at the store and asked him for a ride. What a ride that was. About twenty-five miles per hour and no conversation at all. Hell, the damn thing made too much noise for talking anyway. I forgot that he always stopped to talk to Mrs. Stimson every trip. Folks had been talking about that little stop for years. Well he finally came out and we started on. He let me out at the top of Doane's Hill where I took my suitcase and started down the hill for home. I hoped to pick up a ride but never met a car going either way. About a mile from the house I saw Mrs. Hurd in her front yard and she called out to me to tell me that Mr. Hurd had died and that Dick, her son, had gone into the Marines. I had gone to grade school with Dick, he was two years older than me. He and I had never been close at all but I knew how he felt when his Dad died. I got home in about an hour and of course no one was there. They came in later and were glad to see me. The two weeks went fast and before I could think I found myself back in Gardner waiting for my September call up.

The year before my senior year, Ken and I along with Bob Chase had gone deer hunting and stayed at the farm. We slept three in a bed as our side of the farm was cold as hell. We forgot an alarm clock and tied up some pots and pans with a string and hung them from the bedroom door. The string went through a candle and when it burned down everything would come and it would wake us up. We had to play cards an extra hour to see how long it took for the candle to burn an inch. The damn thing worked and we woke up to one hell of a crash. We were in the woods at first light and had sneaked all the way up to the old Metcalf place which was only a cellar hole in the woods. We were together and trying to decide how to work it when three deer jumped up behind the cellar hole and crossed the cart path in front of us. What a barrage we opened up, and that’s all it was. I think they are still going but we scared the hell out of them. We snarled at each other because we all knew it was not our fault the damn deer had just been too fast. If we could have had it happen again we would have got all three. We hunted just that day and they were the only deer we saw.

I don't thing Margie's father was pleased with me as a potential son in law. Looking at it with a little perspective, I don't blame him but it was a different time and everything was on fast track. Her mother was a real character, but I think she liked me.

Marge's sister Barb was not behaving herself. Her husband was in the Marines and she knew that I knew she was fooling around and expected me to keep quiet about it. I hated to be in that position but did not see any way out. She and another married girl friend were cheating on their husbands together and were slipping around with an old boyfriend of Barb's and his friend, a local fireman. Those two charming gentlemen even took nude pictures of them. I don't think Barb was over bright because she even showed Marge and I and, of course, somehow, they got loose and were passed around the factory. She kept them in a small keyed box on her dresser. Somehow her mother found out where they were and broke open the box. The atmosphere around the house was pretty rough for a few weeks. Margie and I tried our best not to get involved. As far as I know the whole thing was kept from her dad and her husband. Even though her mother had caught her, she stepped out again and I caught her and she begged me to keep quiet. This was putting way too much pressure on me and I told her I'd tell her husband if she didn't stop. I met him overseas the next year and had a hard time not telling him. I've always wondered if I did the right thing. They did not have a very pleasant life and got divorced and he almost killed himself with liquor.

Mother had rented Grammy's side of the house to a family by the name of Hardy. Paul Hardy, the father, had had polio and his legs were almost useless and he had made two canes for himself that went into tripod shape and he got around that way. I never met a nicer man in my life. He was not only nice but he was very well read and very intelligent. His wife was one of the Hamlet girls and he had two boys. The oldest was my age and an alright guy. Paul raised chickens and capons for market and they were great. My junior year I had arranged for him to have two chickens ready for Margie's mother to have for Christmas. The weather was not predicted as it is today and it looked as if there would be only a little snow the day before Christmas. The radio did not predict what it turned into. The day before Christmas, Margie and her mother and I got into the car and we took off for Royalston to get the chickens. It got worse and worse and I started to get worried as I knew the plows in Royalston never got out until the next day. When we got there, there was about a foot of snow on the ground at the farm. We got the chickens and took off for home. I knew if I made the corner by the mail boxes, I would be home free as there was a tar road and if I was careful we could get home. At the corner, you had to go up a short hill and turn left on to the main road. I got the car going as fast as I could, of course with Margie's mother bitching about it, and tried to make the turn. Hell no, stuck, now I mean stuck, couldn't go forward or back. In the back of the car there was dead silence, well at least she was shut up. I didn't know what to do but knew I had to do something.

The only thing I could think of was to go down the road to Aunt Lucy's and ask Levi if he would hitch up the team and pull me out, if not I was dead, maybe literally. How I hated to do it. I only had on dress shoes and it was a half mile to Aunt Lucy's. Off I went leaving words of good cheer and hope. I don't even think anyone even grunted in the back. It just wasn't my day. The snow was worse than ever. You could hardly see ten feet in front and I almost walked by the farm house. I saw a glow and turned into the driveway and up onto the porch and knocked. Aunt Lucy opened the door and the glow that I had seen was from a kerosene lamp, they had lost their power. I told Aunt Lucy what my problem was and she turned to Levi and he looked just thrilled. He said he didn't know if the team could pull me out or not but he would try. He said for me to go back to the car and he would be along as soon as he could. I never felt so guilty in my life. He sounded as if he had a cold and looked awful. I don't know if his son George helped him harness the team but I hope so. It was one hell of a night.

It seemed worse on the way back and when I got there it was very quiet in the car. I tried to make conversation but soon gave up, they just were not having anything to do with me until I got them home. I thought he would never get there and in the meantime the snow was getting deeper and deeper. He finally arrived and I got soaked and so did he trying to find something to hook up to. We got it hooked up and I started the engine and he took up the slack and said go and we went. The horses just pulled me out of there and I was on the road. Levi unhooked and I yelled thank you out the window and took off. There was very little conversation on the way home except some very derogatory remarks on my driving which I didn't think was very fair as I had just saved their lives, or maybe it was mine I had saved. All my life I have felt that I should have gone back and brought Levi a gift or my profound thanks in person. I have been ashamed of the way I treated the help I received that night. Over the years I have thought many times of Levi walking home after he got me free, all alone in the snow and cold then unharnessing the horses and rubbing them down. I wonder if he had gone in and said to Aunt Lucy, "Well I got the little shit out."

That last year in school I had gone back to Kelly's and stuffed cushions after school. I hated the whole thing but we needed all the help we could get. I knew that I would be getting my draft call soon as I had reached eighteen in May. I don't think any young folks tried to make any real plans as the future was pretty hard to predict. I floated through the school year. I had two periods woodworking and had a study period that I spent with Dean helping him in class with the freshmen. I was in a play for the music club. Well really a musical, Robin Hood, it was terrible as the lead just couldn't stay on pitch. All of us wondered how our new music teacher could stand it, but he seemed to think it was great. It was a lot of fun but the way the lead sang was embarrassing. HOW-SOME-EVER it didn't seem to bother him or our music teacher. The lead's father was a very influential man in town and most of us figured our teacher was trying to make points with dear old Dad. Well maybe it helped him in the long run. He had come in after Cogan had his unforgivable indiscretion and was fired. Personally, I always thought Cogan should have done jail time. I don't know what or where he ended up. He just seemed to fade away in the confusion of rumor. I remember I had a solo and believe me I was on key.

Ken and I hunted partridge the year before and did fairly well but the birds seemed not as plentiful this year. I went up to camp with Don and Bob Bridges that fall and got a deer who tried to fly past me on the side hill back of camp. It was a doe that weighed about one twenty and my first one. I caught hell from the Principal as I always did every year for not going to school. I tried not to take it to heart and not to wise off. Well, May came and I got my call to go into the service. I had to report September tenth in Boston.

Graduation was a big event but a little subdued because of the war. I heard that there were a few rather wild times and some drinking, but for me it was rather calm. I never saw or heard of much drinking or of any drugs of any kind. Smoking was about our biggest sin, plus a bit of sex. Margie and I went to the senior prom. It was held in the city hall auditorium and it went very well with very minor problems. The class had one hundred and forty-one members including many that were in the service and two that were killed in action.

I think all of us would have felt very different if the war had been over. As it was now you really didn't know if you were starting a new life or getting ready to lose the one you had.

Margie came up for last two weeks that summer. Dick Hurd who lived about a half mile down the dirt road from me came home from boot camp from the Marines and told me a lot of what I found out later was bullshit. I never saw him in the Corps when I was there. He was discharged early and I always wondered why. My sophomore year I was asked to take a part in a play for Royalston Day and played a butler with a very big part and enjoyed it immensely. The play was very well liked and they put it on later in the fall after I was gone. I always thought it would have been fun to see someone else play my part. Mother said my replacement did very well. It was a great play for me as I had gone to school with most of the cast.

It was my junior year after Ken and I finished cutting the hay that Mother came up with an idea for the four of us to take a trip up to the White Mountains for four days. Aunty was visiting with her friends and we had the use of her car. It sounded like a great idea to all and we took sleeping bags and took off. We had very little money to see anything that you had to pay to see, and we had to sleep out. Mother slept in the car each night and we boys on the ground. We were very careful to pick what we would pay for and discussed each place along the way. The first thing we did was to go on the Ariel Tramway which in the winter was used for a ski lift. It was very high and quite a thrill and was worth the money. We stopped at Ed Clark's Eskimo Ranch to see the dogs and the bears. We went through the Flume which is a series of spectacular waterfalls and didn't cost very much. We saw the Old Man of the Mountain and Profile Lake and all in all had a fine time. There were places to camp out along the way and we took advantage of them when we could.

There was no charge in those days to camp out in these little State camp grounds. We would build a little fire and cook supper every night.

We didn't get our money's worth once at a place called Mystery Lake. It was near North Conway and we saw the sign and it looked like it would be interesting and the price was right. It consisted of a ride on a little lake in a glass bottomed boat and we were told there was an old boat under the water that no one could identify and it was thought to be from early explorers, also the fish were supposed to be different here. Well we all got into the boat and off we went. There were several boats out at the same time. Well the man rowing the boat had a little talk for us as he rowed along. He took us over a group of stumps that were covered with moss and told us how rare they were. They looked the same as they did on Long Pond at home but we just looked at each other and waited for something rare or whatever. He fed the fish and they were all regular Horn Pout and not very big either. After a while he rowed over an old rotten dory of average size. I saw boats like that every spring at the pond that had got loose and sunk in the spring flood.

He kept rowing over old moss-covered logs and tried to make us think they were something special. Finally, we got back to the dock, Mother looked like she was going to explode any second and we tried to leave before she did. We almost made it but the owner who had told us that he had discovered this little spot came after us and wanted to know how we liked it and had we ever seen anything like it before. I kept Mother moving as fast as I could but there were a lot of people coming down the path and this loud mouth kept right behind us trying to get Mother to say something. I wanted to tell him to shut up and not press his luck. Well he got his wish. All of a sudden Mother stopped all traffic and turned around and said, "I'll tell you exactly what I saw, I saw some very ordinary horn pout, a half a dozen old logs and an old rotten row boat. Seeing you asked and insist on knowing what I think of the whole thing, I'll tell you. I think that this whole place is the biggest rip off in the White Mountains and you should be put out of business." The whole line of potential customers stopped and a large share turned around and started to walk back up the path toward their cars. The man with the big mouth and inquiring mind was very upset and tried to stop the exodus. One man turned to him and grinned and said, "Well you asked her." I was so embarrassed but I really shouldn't have been. Mother was right. The only mystery was how he got away with the whole thing.

That was our last day and we headed for home. It was a fine trip and one I will always remember as it was the last time we all got together like that. I'll tell you one thing, do not mess with my mother unless you know you are very capable of defending yourself. Obviously, he didn't have that capability. That was a great summer.

My daughter just sent me a picture of the log cabin that Ken and I built along with our best friend Bob. It was right after Dad had died and we needed something to take our minds off feeling sorry for ourselves. Ken and I had talked for years about building a cabin in the woods in what we called the mill yard. We had even picked a spot. There was an old cart path that led off to the right of our dirt road where maybe a hundred years ago logs had been stacked to go to the mill. About a quarter mile down the old path on the right there was a big stand of very straight pine trees. They were all about seven inches thick at the butt and we thought we could cut at least three big twelve-foot logs from each that would have very little taper. Ken and I showed Bob the spot and he thought it would be perfect and wanted to start immediately. Our best friend, Bob, was always ready for whatever we came up with. Bob and I sharpened up our two-man crosscut saw and we started to cut the trees. Bob and I cut the trees and cut them into logs twelve feet long. Ken trimmed off the branches. We really had not thought about a foundation, and Ken said why not cut a really big tree and use that for a base. That was the best idea we could think of, so Bob and I cut a big pine about twelve inches at the butt and cut it into logs thirteen feet long. We had a hell of a time moving them into place making them level and square, but after about a day we did it. There was about thirty big rough sawn four by fours that had never been sold and they had been stacked down behind the barn and we figured they would make great inside corners. We thought maybe we could spike the logs to them.

When Mom had settled the Whitfield estate, Ken and I had found a whole keg of very rusty old spikes. We didn't know what to do with them so we just stuck them in the barn. I have no idea what they were made for but they were ten inches long and as our logs were only six inches thick, they would be perfect. Well we had a foundation, a level, and a square, so what were we waiting for? We put up four posts 4" inch by four" as corner posts and off we went. We left a place for a door and Ken found an old chicken coop window and we left a spot for it. Luckily there was enough old boards around to do the roof. It sure wasn't much but we were proud of it. We always intended to put in a floor and hang a door but never did. Thirty years later when I went in to see it, it was gone. In my mind, it's still there. I can't remember who took the picture but all three of us are in it, even our dog Dick. My oldest son Gary remembers walking in the old cart path and seeing it.

The day came, I said goodbye to Mom, Aunty and Ken, took the train for Boston and joined the Marines, but that's another story.

My brother passed away December 30, 2016. Ken was two years younger than me. He and his wife Doris lived within site of the farm where we were both born. He bought the Shepardson Farm from Aunt Lucy and Levi with all its fields and woods. That leaves me as the last of the Royalston Stewarts. I've tried to tell about how it was for Ken and I growing up through the depression and going to school in a one room school house. Was it a better time? Damned if I know but it was our time and I think we both took it to heart. Sons, daughters, grandkids, nieces, nephews, cousins, that's the way it was.

I turned ninety one May 20, 2017. Perhaps I should have left out the facts about John's death, but it made a very deep impression on me growing up. I never discussed it with Dan as by the time I knew the facts it seemed pointless.

Written on Cape Cod by Arthur Eri Stewart, age ninety-one, May 20, 2017.

AUTHOR'S BIO

Arthur Eri Stewart is a World War II Marine veteran who served in the Pacific. At 92, he is retired after a career as a building contractor. He was born in rural Royalston, MA and has lived on Cape Cod for over 45 years. He served as the Building Inspector in Orleans for three years. An avid sportsman, Arthur is a trapshooter, hunter, fisherman and birdwatcher. He has three sons and a daughter and the stories in this book animated many a conversation. In addition to *Hilltop Echoes*, Arthur is the author of three novels: *The Highwayman*, *Jessie's Legacy* and *Last Haven Follies*. He is currently working on a novel based on his experiences in the Marine Corp.

CPSIA information can be obtained
at www.ICGtesting.com
Printed in the USA
BVHW041621140522
636930BV00001B/93

9 781605 710266